Lucius

by Matthew Lieberman

"With malice toward none...."

-Abraham Lincoln

"What white people have to do is try to find out in their hearts why it was necessary for them to have a nigger in the first place. Because I am not a nigger. I'm a man.... If you invented him, you the white people invented him, then you have to find out why. And the future of the country depends on that."

-James Baldwin

"I learned a long time ago that reality was much weirder than anyone's imagination."

-Hunter S. Thompson

Part One - The River

Chapter 1

I sit down to write this story today, intentionally, on my fiftieth birthday. On a metric scale of time, I'd be exactly halfway between born and dead. It's kind of fun to imagine myself at this halfway point, this fulcrum, with fifty actual years behind me and fifty imaginary years ahead. I can sit here in Atlanta, in the halfway house of my life, and wonder which side of this bar will grow heavier as I keep along the inch by inch journey towards dead. I'll be going down that unrealized road, and as I get closer to dead you'd think the scale would tip in that direction, slowly until the terminal day. And yet the length of time behind me will grow longer and longer, so maybe the scale will finally fall to that side, back to born. I realize this could sound like religion, and I only mean it as speculation. For many years now, I've been happy enough to let the unknown be the unknown.

I sit here in Atlanta in my house on the Chattahoochee River in the year 2017. I was born in 1967. In 1949 George Orwell wrote *1984*, which I read in 1981 in eighth grade. In 1968 Stanley Kubrick directed *2001: A Space Odyssey*, which the theatrical release posters described as "an epic drama of adventure and exploration." I've lived in a time and place, these fifty years in the United States of America, that seem to have outrun time, outpaced even epic adventure.

And yet I sit here on a river which Union and Confederate soldiers warred over in 1864 during Sherman's March to the Sea. The river, which rolls past my back yard, was the last physical barrier between the Union and Atlanta. An important pontoon bridge was laid across the river not fifty yards from my lawn. Hourly, I hear trains whistling by a mile downstream on the old Western and Atlantic railroad tracks, an important supply line of those battles. On July 4, 1864 Union forces commanded by General Sherman defeated Confederate forces commanded by General Johnston. This was The Battle of Vining's Station. Union forces crossed the river, on July 22 the Battle of Atlanta commenced, the city was besieged and then fell on September 2, 1864. The

Confederate States surrendered in April of 1865, and by June of that year all slaves had been freed.

I was on a plane from New York back to Atlanta yesterday. Next to me sat two people, a young man and woman, perhaps a couple. He was somewhat pudgy, not tall, probably Jewish, wearing thick-framed hipster eyeglasses. She was slight, brown skinned, and pretty in a mild way. His physical movements suggested they were a couple, but there was nothing blatant, and they could have been friends or work colleagues. A lot of movies are filmed in Atlanta now, and the two of them could easily have been a part of that world -- a guy and his assistant, a woman and hers, two equals on the project. It was hard to tell. To my eye, it seemed she could do better, but maybe he was producing the whole project and worth millions, or hooked up to a non-extravagant but steady trust fund drip from his parents' or grandparents' veins into his which was sufficient to make him attractive. Without asking it was impossible to say. She was watching *Gone with the Wind* on the seatback screen in front of her. I've tried to watch it once or twice, but the overripe accents and pathos and length do me in. She was listening through her earbuds, so I couldn't hear, but I found it interesting to watch. Or watch her watching. It looked different to me, maybe because the accents weren't in play, or maybe because I couldn't help see things a little bit like she might be seeing them. Or wonder what it all looked like to her. Fancy, overwrought Whites; noble yet pathetic slave Blacks; Confederate stars and bars; antebellum plantation life; old Atlanta. I realize now that her being Black and him being White was the least interesting thing about the whole arrangement. It raised the fewest questions in my mind. The more granular interested me more: what she saw in him, what she saw in the movie, what his actual deal was. The fact that they were different races was merely obvious.

Not long ago, such a pairing wouldn't just have been interesting but sensational, daring, transgressive. And not too long before that, it would have been illegal in the South. Maybe if they were my age, the racial difference would have been more surprising. Probably. But a twenty-something White dude and twenty-something Black woman flying from liberal, diverse New York City, to the liberal city of Atlanta which is half Black in 2017 doesn't raise my eyebrow. Black, White, gay, straight, and everything in between -- unremarkable. That said, the woman next to me could have flipped the seatback screen from *Gone with the Wind* to CNN and seen the same Confederate flags along with swastikas and torches all on the march, on the move, in liberal Charlottesville, Virginia and be confirmed in the belief that the long gone and far away never left and are close at hand.

I am White and from the North. I grew up and lived my first three and a half decades in New Haven, Connecticut, a liberal northeastern city, a college town. I am Jewish and carry the additional progressive attitudes still characteristic of most Jews who can't help but to identify as The Other and with The Other. I grew up on a bible that teaches kindness to the stranger because we were once strangers in a strange land, that reminds Jews of our own long, slave experience and that man was not created to be a beast owned by another man and forced to bear that other man's burden. I also grew up in a country I love and that is mine. I swallowed my dose of *e pluribus unum* whole. I hold these truths to be self-evident. But in 2017 it is just as self-evident that many Americans don't. They hold different truths, and the instinct to subjugate or even kill as they deem necessary. The jackboots are marching on American soil. It feels like we've outlived history and have begun to full-cycle repeat it.

I have a story to tell, an unlikely story. It's a story of love, and it's a story of hope. One of the people is Black; the other, White.

One is a slave; the other, a slaveholder. My friend, the White man, is named Benno Johnson. His slave, now gone from Benno's world, was named Lucius Cincinnatus Jones.

My name is Tree Weissman. My parents didn't name me Tree. That came the way of nicknames. My given name is Mordecai Weissman. When I was born in 1967, Mordecai was not amongst the names in vogue. Those were days of Michaels and Davids and Jeffreys. Nonetheless my parents were of their own minds around the margins of the truly important, and they were willing to tread those margins when it came to their son's name. So I was named Mordecai, and Mordecai I was called until around fifth grade.

I grew up in a bygone day when boys collected baseball cards, studied the statistics on the backs of those cards, and learned the names and records of the all-time greats from the official recorded annals of the game. This history work was a mainstream hobby, not a school assignment, and simple souls that we were, we enjoyed it. So at around age ten, I came across the name and personage of one of the ancient greats, Mordecai "Three Finger" Brown. Mordecai Brown was born in rural Indiana in 1876, America's centennial year, and in fact his full name was Mordecai Peter Centennial Brown. I supposed that the name Mordecai was probably more common in that old, far off time, but the presence of Centennial in his full name gave me another link to this all-time great -- the link of slightly cockeyed parentage. I couldn't imagine that Centennial was ever a name sound-minded parents would give a child, even in the centennial year. America's bicentennial had just passed, and no one I knew had named or middle-named a child Bicentennial, so I was pretty sure his parents were a bit cracked, like mine.

And he was an all-time great! The nickname Three Finger stemmed from a farm machinery accident when he was eleven in which he lost parts of two of his fingers. Sometimes the universe recompenses the sufferer, and this was such a time. His unique finger arrangement led to a uniquely sharp breaking curveball which led to a life-time record of 239 wins against 130 losses, an earned run average of 2.06, and 1,375 career strikeouts. Mordecai Brown, Mordecai Weissman -- pretty cool. Of course, my friends fastened on to the part of his name more colorful than Mordecai. So instead of Mordecai they called me Three Finger. Which wasn't so bad, but wasn't so good either. Fortunately, it soon shortened to Three, and then, because I was tall for a ten-year-old, Tree. Which is actually a pretty damn good name.

I met Benno Johnson two spring times ago through my volunteering at our city's Jewish Home for the Elderly. This was unlikely in two ways: first, Benno wasn't Jewish; and second, I really don't like volunteering. Yes, I've served on boards from time to time when asked. I own some real estate; it was my business that brought me to Atlanta. What I own is mostly strip malls, nothing too big, but enough to have a decent income rolling in each year and to say yes when asked for a check. There are many bigger players in the Atlanta Jewish world. I like to stay under the radar, do my modest but appreciated thing, and mind my own business. Honestly, I don't have a lot of energy for community work. I like the community, respect the people who give it a lot of time, but have concluded that I'm not going to be one of them. Most days I walk my dog, do some non-taxing work for my business, take a nap, think about playing golf, take another nap, and then have a drink, make dinner, walk the dog again, watch some TV, and hit the hay. I've been married a couple times, have a couple kids I love who are now out of the house, have lived in this house a couple years since the end of my second marriage, and pretty much have liberty, along with my dog, to do whatever. If this liberty sounds like it could be lonely, well, sometimes it is. And while it wasn't loneliness that led me to the Home, or Benno, something to do with being alone is probably part of what drew me to Benno's story.

I have a good voice, and through the years I learned to lead parts of the Jewish prayer service at synagogue. The chaplain at the Jewish home heard I had this skill from his son who is a member of my congregation. He needed people to run Sabbath services for the residents on Saturday mornings. It wasn't easy to find people who would do this. Many people were capable, but due to a variety of Jewish legal rules, it wasn't practical for these people to get there. I had relaxed my adherence to these rules a little bit over the years, so I could get there. I could get there, I knew how to lead services, they needed someone to do this, I knew it was a good deed, I had no real reason but shameful laziness to say no, so I said yes. I was happy to do it because I knew it was the right thing to do. But I wasn't excited about it. And old people make me uncomfortable because I expect them to die, in the near term, and I don't want to be there when it happens. I realize this is not a completely rational aversion, but it's not completely irrational either. The clock is ticking, systems are failing, and it becomes a game of odds.

As I said, Benno wasn't Jewish. The Jewish Home was open to members of other faiths, but non-Jews were in the minority.

Nonetheless, Benno seemed to have a lot of friends, or at least an audience, that enjoyed his personality and his stories. Of course, they thought he was crazy. The fact that he claimed to have owned a slave for most of his life certainly figured in the collective assessment of his mental health. While the residents of the Home were all old and failing in one way or another, and while many of them said things that were jumbled, or not fully rooted in fact, claiming, as Benno did, to have owned a slave through most of the twentieth century and the start of the twenty-first -- well, that stood out. Nevertheless, he seemed otherwise mentally acute. And he was also fun to be around -- a true and big-hearted character.

As a non-Jew, Benno didn't come to services. Most of the residents didn't. I had a group of twenty "congregants" most weeks. It wasn't an official congregation or synagogue, and I'm not an official or even unofficial rabbi, so I won't call them official congregants. But around twenty souls showed up each week. Some sang along, some held eye contact with me when I'd look their way, some dozed off. Some looked happy to be there, even excited, like they'd been looking forward to it; others I would place on the positive end of the neutral scale, and a couple looked like their parents made them come. I led the service out of a laminated and spiral bound abbreviation of the full prayer book. It included only the Sabbath service, not the services for every day or the holidays. Still, it took an hour and fifteen minutes from beginning to end including a brief thought I would offer on the weekly torah reading. Sometimes this five-minute ramble would actually sound like a sermon with a beginning, a middle, and a message or moral at the end. More often, it was truly just a thought, at the end of which I'd say something like "All right, there you go." I believe the thoughts were generally good thoughts, but as I've said I am not a rabbi, so I didn't feel any rabbinical obligation to the standard form.

We met in what was really a lovely multipurpose room. While the carpeting and walls were standard office building issue, the ceiling was probably twenty-five feet high, and through the small windows behind me and larger windows to my right and left, the sun poured in the mid-morning light. Also, the Home had installed a very beautiful wooden ark, maple stained, to hold the torah scroll. I stood in front of the ark as I led services, looking back at five rows of chairs and the door to the room through which we had all entered.

I met Benno because this door was left opened. My voice is not small, and as I've said, it's pretty good. My daughters, who also have good voices and who seldom compliment me unnecessarily, actually think I could have been a cantor. I (but not so much they) think I could've made a run at a Broadway career. In any event, I'm not bad and my voice, even unamplified, carries. More than once on my way out, the greeter at the reception desk which is probably thirty-five feet outside the room where we meet, in which I stand probably twenty feet from the door, has told me how she so enjoys listening to my voice and that it really carries with great warmth out into the lobby. Which I'm happy to hear because I'm not there to shout at the people or set them to fiddling with their hearing aids. There's a time to belt, and a time to modulate. And even the hard of hearing appreciate some nuance.

The lobby of the home looks like a welcoming hotel lobby in the style of southern lodges. There's a Ritz Carlton ninety minutes away at Reynolds Plantation, and the lobby of the Home, while not full-on luxurious, points in that direction. It's nice, with comfortable couches and matching armchairs in happy, warm autumnal hues. I would venture that an additional five or ten residents half attended services each week sitting in this lovely lobby.

It was while leaving one Saturday late morning, as I traversed the lobby to the sliding glass front doors, that I first heard Benno's voice.

"Rabbi!" It came out sounding halfway between rabbi and ribeye.

"Yessir!"

"C'mon over here, Rabbi."

"Alrighty." Instead of exiting, I walked past the sliding entrance doors to that half of the lobby. I realized that in all the times I'd come in and out of the Home, I'd never been on that side of the lobby. I would enter, turn right, and directly proceed to the room where I led services. I'd exchanged greetings with some of my lobby-sitting half congregants on the way in and out, but that was all.

Benno was arrayed in one of the comfortable looking stuffed armchairs and motioned for me to sit down at the end of the couch next to him. Two other residents sat in the same seating area, and out the side of my eye, I caught their expressions which hung on arched eyebrows somewhere between amusement and concern.

"But you know, in full disclosure, I need to tell you I'm not a rabbi," I said.

"Not a rabbi?!" He was somewhere between upset, incensed, and, I could tell, just playing with me. "Then what are you?!"

"Well, someone I know told the chaplain that I knew how to lead services, so I just come in to help out."

"Hmm. So you're a *do-gooder*." He made it sound a little sinister, "You go around doing good things."

"Thank you," I said. "When I can't find a reason not to, I guess I sometimes do."

"I see. Very modest. Very modest. Hmm. So you're not a rabbi. Well, that's okay because I'm not a Jew! Is there a Jewish word for do-gooder? I think there is. What's that word. Pearl?"

Pearl was one of the others sitting with us. "Mensch."

"Mensch! That's it. Thank you, Pearl. Pearl speaks good Jewish."

"Yiddish," she corrected.

"Yiddish. Yes." And then to me in a stage whisper she couldn't hear, "I think they mean the same thing, Yiddish and Jewish. Am I right, Rabbi?" Though there are differences, I nodded. He continued, "Yeah, but I'm not Yiddish or Jewish, so I defer to Pearl." And now louder, "I'm a stranger in a strange land, Rabbi! A stranger in a strange land."

I could tell this last statement of his had pleased him. His manner was open and immediately ingratiating. I held out my hand.

"My name's Tree Weissman."

"Tree Weissman! I grew up with a Tree Weissman!"

"You did?"

"No! Of course not." His deadpan was convincing; for a moment my world tilted on its special axis at the thought of another Tree Weissman. "Tree Weissman? That can't be your real name."

"You're correct. My real name is Mordecai."

"Mordecai. That's more like it. Mordecai. I'm Benno, by the way. Benno Johnson. So tell me. How'd you get Tree from Mordecai?"

My usual answer was "because I'm tall," but there was something about Benno's open manner that invited the longer form response, so I gave it to him.

"I like it. I do. Tree Weissman. Good name. But Mordecai - - that's a great name. Mordecai from the Book of Esther if I'm not mistaken. Isn't that right, Pearl?" He looked over at her.

"What's that, Benno?"

"Mordecai was in the story of Esther, am I right?"

"Yes, the story of Esther."

"I know my bible," he said. "Yes, I do. Know *all* my testaments. Mordecai wouldn't bow to the evil Haman, so Haman got the King to order the death of Mordecai and all the Jews. Haman was at that time the King's main counselor, the Persian term being 'Numero Uno,' and the King was slow on the uptake, so he would just go along. He had many wives, but his favorite happened to be the ravishing Jewess, Esther. And Esther happened to be the niece of Mordecai. Am I right, Mordecai?"

"You are," I said. As he spun out his faithful synopsis of the Book of Esther, I noticed he had a very expressive, physical way of talking. His hands, his posture, the angle of his head, the movements of his eyebrows, and how open or slitted he held his eyes -- sometimes it was like he was conducting an orchestra; sometimes, like he was examining a witness, his hands moving in lines and circles. It was fun to watch.

"So Mordecai asked, no verily *beseeched* Esther to intercede on behalf of her people with the King, which she did. And instead of Mordecai, it was Haman who ended up dead. And all his sons. And the children of Israel were saved once again," he concluded, his hands temporarily coming to rest. "Do you mind if I call you Mordecai? I haven't called anyone Mordecai in a long, long time."

It didn't bother me, and in any event I didn't think I'd be spending much time with Benno, so I said fine. And then, very solemn, he said this:

"My slave, Lucius, he always told me his daddy's name was Mordecai. I never met Mordecai, but Lucius, he held his daddy's memory in *reverence*, what he could remember of him, from when he was a little boy." Benno had been looking in my direction, but it was clear he had gone to somewhere else. After a moment passed he focused and saw what must have been a look of concern on my face. "Oh!" he continued, more in his previous tone and bright manner. "I haven't told you about Lucius. How about you stay after services next week. I'll treat you to lunch here. It's a nice dining room, the food is better than passable and sometimes very good. And we can chat a little more. What do you say, young Mordecai?"

I had never been to the other side of the lobby before that day. I didn't like staying places, and I didn't like feeling I might have to make conversation with people I didn't really know. And as I said, I didn't want to become complicit by my presence in a

20

resident's death. I liked moving on, getting outside that place, going home. And yet I found myself saying yes. Benno was a character. I enjoyed him. And he was going to tell me about his slave, whose father and I shared a name.

"That sounds good. I'll see you here next week."

"Next week."

Chapter 2

Now, dear reader, I know and I knew that with the Emancipation Proclamation and then the end of the Civil War, slavery had ceased to exist in these here United States. That said, Benno clearly had something in mind. Perhaps he was speaking metaphorically, though an odd and impolitic metaphor it would be. Or perhaps he was crazy, delusional, though the entire rest of my first interaction with him belied that broad a diagnosis. I was interested to see exactly what he was talking about, and as the following week passed and Saturday morning neared, I had more on my mind than what my non-sermony sermon would be.

As usual, I arrived at around 10:20 am, ten minutes before we started, to avoid being late. And to avoid being early, I sat in the car for a few minutes before getting out and heading in. As I passed through the sliding glass doors, I couldn't stop myself from cutting a quick glance to my left to see if Benno was there. He wasn't, and I continued my usual short course back to the right and into our makeshift sanctuary. Though he wouldn't necessarily be there an hour and a half before we were set to meet, I did half hope to see him ready and waiting and wondered if maybe he would forget.

My elderly flock occupied my attention for the next seventy-five minutes. The service went well, Sabbath pleasantries were exchanged, and I headed out into the lobby.

"Rabbi Mordecai!" I heard him before I saw him.

"Yessir," I said, locating him across the other side where we'd met the previous week.

"Good to see you. Good Shabbos!" He smiled with satisfaction.

"Thank you. Your Yiddish is spot on."

"I know it. I know it. Survival skills. Your people know about those, aren't I right, Mordecai."

"We do. Too many opportunities to learn them."

"Indeed. Yes, indeed." He got up from his chair carefully and reached out to shake my hand. "Let's head into lunch. It's pretty good. I think you'll like it."

We walked down a hallway towards the dining room. He moved carefully but not stiffly. As we walked, he picked up our short conversational thread.

"Tell me, Mordecai, why do you think your people have drawn so much fire? All the Jew-hating. There's hardly any of you! What'd you do to deserve it?"

Though I wasn't sure if the topic of my ancient negro namesake and that namesake's son, Lucius, would come up, I was aware that Benno's mind hosted these characters, and the "your people" and "deserve it" bits set me on edge for a second. But he seemed to like Jews, and he seemed to like me, so I wrote off his phrasing to his age and withheld judgement.

"What did we do to deserve it? Nothing," I said. "Unless being different or successful is a crime."

"Not a crime, Mordecai. No way, no how."

We were in the dining room now, and Benno walked us over to a table with Pearl and two other lady residents. We sat down and joined them.

"Mordecai, I believe you know Pearl," I nodded. "Meet my friends Hazel and Iris. Hazel and Iris, meet our rabbi, Mordecai."

I assured the ladies I wasn't a rabbi, accepted their compliments for my singing which they said they sometimes listened to from out in the lobby, and we all started telling the server what we would have for lunch. There was a nice-looking buffet on one side of the room, and when the server told us our options and took our orders, she proceeded to collect our lunch and bring it over. In fact, the food was good. Not great, but good. The institutional whiff was inescapable, but it was a square meal and tasty enough to feel you weren't being punished. Probably eighty percent of the servers, and staff generally, were not White, and most of these were Black which I knew was not unusual for a nursing home. Most of these jobs paid $11 or $12 an hour and around $20,000 a year. I'd guess half of the staff had a high school diploma or less. These jobs were difficult, could be outright trying, and paid poorly. But the staff at the Home seemed to be bearing up well enough. And the residents, aside from the old age grouches, were uniformly appreciative and polite. Southerners are polite. Since moving to Atlanta thirteen years ago, I've learned that the stereotype is true. There is a politesse to their formal interactions that smooths out the sharp angles and edges of daily life. This is particularly true of the older generation, but even children speak in the language of "sir" and "ma'am." I've also found that the smiles and savoir faire can be nothing more than smiles and savoir faire. People will gladly screw you just like they will in Connecticut or Colorado or California. For a while, you'll just be more surprised.

Nonetheless, it does keep the social machine humming along, even in a room like this one, where all the Blacks were serving all the Whites -- an aesthetic that tends to jangle my Northern nerves.

Hazel and Iris liked Benno, I could tell. He kept himself in fine fettle. He dressed neatly and well with a touch of old southern prep to his style. And he had maintained his basic exoskeletal structure. All his joints and major body parts were in their original places. No great sagging or dislocation had yet occurred. And he had that easy physicality that especially stood out in a nursing home. What's more, he had a spark in his eye that would appeal to anyone. For an old codger, he wasn't much of a codger. He was a scamp.

The ladies were updating Benno on their grandchildren.

"No, Sophie is a junior already," Iris was saying. "She's a junior at Maryland. She loves it."

"Is she dating?" Hazel asked.

"You know, it seems like they don't date as much. They all seem to do things together. At least that's what she tells me. She *was* dating a boy last year. He's from Atlanta. Maybe she knew him from high school? I met him once. Nice looking boy. Not Jewish, but I think that ended."

"Good," Hazel said.

"Yes, 'good' is right! You know, on the one hand she's young. But on the other hand, she's not so young. They're getting married younger again I think. I watch that wedding dress show on TV, what's it called? It's the one at Kleinfeld's in New York. Do you watch it?"

"Yes, I've seen it."

"Well, I'm forgetting the name, but the brides that come in, some of them are young. Really. Just out of college. I tell Sophie to be careful, take her time. Live a little."

"There's supposed to be a big Jewish population at Maryland," Hazel offered.

"There is! Immense! There are so many things going on with Hillel and the Chabad. It's wonderful. She says she does some of it, but I know it's not really her thing right now. And you know what? That's fine. She should just take her time."

"That's right," said Hazel. "Take her time. That's what I tell my Kayla."

"Is she the one who visited this week?" Iris asked.

"Yes...I mean no! That was Becca. Becca's still in high school. A junior in *high* school I think. Kayla is a sophomore, at Georgia. Wait...no...yes, a sophomore at Georgia."

"Go Dawgs!" Benno interjected. He was content to listen to the ladies, but the mention of Georgia had stirred him.

"That's right, you studied in Athens," said Iris.

Benno laughed a heh-heh laugh. "Studied! I don't know I'd go that far. But I spent four years there. Class of '49. Started right after the war. Great times there. Great times."

I did the math in my head. From his looks, he could have been anywhere from around eighty to around ninety or a bit older I figured. If he was twenty-two in 1949, that meant he was born in 1927. So he was probably ninety. He was doing all right. The ladies continued.

"I don't doubt you had a very fine time in Athens, Benno," Iris said. "My husband told me some wild stories about those days. He was Class of '56."

"Well, it's much more serious now," Hazel chimed in. "The kids were telling me that the SATs of the students now are as good as *Harvard!*"

"That's what I hear," said Iris. "Anyway, 'take your time.' That's what I tell Sophie as well. They all seem so busy with their Snap and Facebook and the other things, and always on their phones -- I don't think a one of them really knows where they're going."

The conversation continued in this vein, Hazel and Iris chit-chatting along, Benno offering a quick nugget now and again. The ladies were talking to each other, but by their manner I could tell they were just as much talking to him. The man was the ladies' audience. And even when silent, Benno's gestures and expressions and laughs kept up his side of the conversation. Shortly after we finished eating, two Black aides came over to help Hazel and Iris to their walkers and then back, I presumed, to their rooms, although the Home offered a full slate of programming, so they could have been off to their next activity as well. In any event, Benno and I remained.

"They're fun," I said.

"Hazel and Iris? Yeah. They're all right, those two. They're good old broads. Listening to ladies talk about the thises and thats -- it's a pleasure of life. One of my favorite things now. And when those granddaughters come to visit, that's not too bad either. If you know what I mean. Easy on the eyes."

"I imagine so. Do you have any grandkids or kids around here?"

"Not around here. And not around there. No kith or kin at all. I'm the last of the Mohicans, son. The last. It was me and Lucius until he passed three years ago, August 16th, the day that Elvis died. Now it's just me."

I resisted the temptation to inquire after the relevance of Elvis to the event, and also held back from pressing the matter of Lucius. I'd learned that in the South more than elsewhere, patience was required and then rewarded with the natural unfolding of the tale, all relevant details included. Between here and there, Elvis and similar such flotsam and jetsam might float by. But it was false bait. "Did you ever have any family here?" I asked.

"I did. I had parents. I'm of woman born, Mordecai. And sired non-immaculately by my father." He winked.

"That's good to hear," I said. "Were you born in Atlanta?"

"I was. Born and bred in Dixie. And my parents before me, also, born and bred here. And so, too, three more generations back to the founding of the city. Do you know what it was called then?"

"Either Marthasville or Terminus, right?"

"It was Terminus. That's correct. The end of the line of the Western and Atlantic Railroad. Then a few years *after* that, Marthasville, after Governor Lumpkin's daughter Martha. And then Atlanta a couple years later. 1845."

"And your people were here all the way back then."

"We were, and we have been. And I'm the last."

"Only child?" I ventured.

"Only child of two only children. My father was Benjamin, and my mother was Rosalyn. They were good parents I'd say, but I don't know I really knew them well. They had a group of friends and did things with their friends. They died in a car wreck my freshman year at Georgia. They were headed to the Cloister for a week and had a wreck around Statesboro. Went off the road."

"Wow. I'm sorry. That's rough. How'd you take care of yourself then?"

"Well, I was already in college, so day in day out I was already on my own with Lucius. And they left enough of an estate so that I didn't have to worry. They owned a lot of land here since the beginning. So between rents and selling off pieces, I was always fine."

"That's good."

"Yes, that's been better than good, Mordecai. Now understand, I haven't been *altogether* shiftless. I got a law degree in Athens as well, and I practiced some. Wills and trusts and now and then getting a golf buddy off the hook for exercising his constitutional right to be stupid. But the practice of law, if I'm going to be honest with you, was mostly window dressing."

"Window dressing?" I asked.

"To keep me looking respectable. Kinda like the city version of being a gentleman farmer. You've heard the nickname "The city too busy to hate?"

"Yes."

"Well, in 'The city too busy to hate,' it's good to look like you might be doing something. So I practiced law, but not too hard."

"Sounds reasonable."

There was a pause as this narrative line concluded. We had wandered away from Lucius, but, again, I felt it was poor form to just come out and ask about him. The social code affords men less room to be gossipy or to pry. Whether asking an old man in 2017 about his recently departed slave is technically prying, I can't say for sure. It might be more like playing make believe. But unless they're at strip clubs or on the golf course, grown men aren't really allowed to do that either. A lovely southern woman my age would just out and say "Now, Benno, honey, you were going to tell me more about *Lucius*, your *slave*." To which he might have responded, "Aw, I don't know, sugar, there's not much to say really." To which she might have responded by softly but not too softly taking his old hand in her younger, rose and lilac scented one, and saying, "Go *on*, you silly man! *Tell* me. You can't dangle something like that out there and not *tell* me," and then seductively leaning in with a slice of cleavage to the fore, "Tell me." And he'd tell her.

That routine is not in the male playbook. So we had a little pause. Benno asked an aide for a cup of coffee. "Would you like some coffee?" he asked me.

"Thank you. Yes."

"How do you like it?" the aide asked.

"Just black, thank you."

"Regular or decaf."

"Regular, thanks."

"Black coffee!" chimed Benno. "I like that, Mordecai. Pretty stout. Pretty stout stuff, son!" And then to the aide, "You know mine, Darlin', light and sweet. I drank mine black into my eighties, but I've gone soft."

"I never drank coffee until around ten years ago," I told him. "Then I was in Miami on vacation with my second wife, and I tried some with her at a Latin restaurant in Miami Beach and discovered I'd developed a taste for it."

I realized I'd actually just led us down a tributary potentially filled with flotsam and jetsam myself -- coffee, tea, other beverages; Miami, Latin America, other destinations; my second wife, my first wife, my relationship almanac. I really hadn't shared anything with him about any of this, or about my own professional life, which, like the one he had, afforded the blessing and curse of free time. And to the extent I was in real estate and he'd been clipping coupons his whole adult life from his family's own real estate holdings, we had a livelihood more or less in common. But I wasn't going to go down that path. I was pissed as it was that I'd introduced the topic of liking coffee.

Fortunately, Benno seemed preoccupied and only said, in a drifting kind of way, "Yes...Miami Beach...Supposed to be very nice...Very nice....Good coffee...," he trailed off. I grabbed the chance to steer us back.

"'The city too busy to hate,' where did that nickname come from?" I asked. It was a question I already knew the answer to, and I knew it would set Benno on a path back to Lucius.

"The Sixties!" He snapped back into focus. "Our mayor then, Ivan Allen, Jr., and the business establishment, wanted Atlanta to look modern, keep growing, stay open for business. We didn't want to get bogged down in race problems like other Southern cities. Now, that doesn't mean people here liked all the civil rights stuff any more than the folks did in Montgomery, or Little Rock, or Jackson, Mississippi. It just means that the 'haves' liked having, and they were smart enough to see they could be having a lot more if they kept things calm and friendly. And I guess they did a good job of it. We weren't much bigger than Birmingham back then. Maybe not bigger at all. And look now. I don't know that we've ever been more righteous than anyone else. Just smarter."

The coffees came, and we thanked the aide. Benno took a careful sip. "Mmm. Hot. Good." And then, "So look, I invited you over today to tell you about me and Lucius. Did you know that's how I ended up here -- a little bit after Lucius died, my neighbors called up social services because they thought I'd gone mad."

"Why?"

"Oh, hell, you know. You see an old man sitting by the river all night talking to it, you think he's crazy."

"You were talking to the river?"

"No! I wasn't talking to the river. I was talking to Lucius. I was *sitting* by the river. I was *talking* to Lucius. But that explanation didn't help things out much either."

"Because you said he was your slave?"

"No! I didn't get to that part. *You* try sitting by the river all night talking to someone who's not there. Your neighbors will probably call you out on it, too. Don't even have to be ancient like me. No, I understood it. There aren't too many people my age living on their own in a big house to start with. There wasn't an argument I could make. And truth is, without Lucius, I was lonely. I didn't mind the thought of having some people around."

I was trying hard at this point not to jump on the fact that he said he lived by the river. There weren't that many houses in Atlanta that were on the river, and the probability that he had lived near where I live -- well, I had to remind myself that it was besides the point. "I can see how you'd be lonely."

"Hell, yes! I'm not ashamed to say it. I'm too old to have that kind of ego. And it's the God's truth."

"How long was Lucius with you?" I was aware of sounding vaguely like a psychiatrist or intake coordinator.

"Since I can't remember when, that's how long. As long as I can remember, Mordecai." His tone and visage saddened.

"You told me his father's name was also Mordecai?"

"That's right. That's what he told me. I don't know that I ever met his daddy. I think he may have grown up working on my family's land in one way or another. I'm not positive of that. Not positive. But Lucius spoke of him fondly."

"So Lucius left him to come with you?"

"That's right. Or actually, it may have been that his daddy died, and my parents gave Lucius to me. He never talked about his mother, so he must not have ever really known her. In any event, he showed up and from then on we were always together."

"He was your slave."

"Yes. I remember. I said, 'So you're my slave,' and he said 'Yes, Massa.'"

"Massa is what he called you?"

"Yes. Massa. Or Massa Benno. Sometimes Sir, like 'Yessuh.' And I called him Lucius. His full name was Lucius Cincinnatus Jones."

"Lucius Cincinnatus Jones?"

"Quite a name, isn't it? Lucius Cincinnatus was a Roman figure of ancient times. And then there was also a Confederate politician Lucius Cincinnatus Lamar. Most likely that's the link. And I suppose he came to us from a Jones family. But yes, Lucius Cincinnatus Jones. Of course, I never gave that any thought at all at the time. "

"And how old were you?"

"Well, that was a long time ago. I was probably eight or nine years old, and Lucius always seemed about the same age as me. We were young, and like I told you, one day, there he was, and he was my slave. We both knew that. We used to walk around the house together, inseparable, like he was my pup. I remember my parents liked Lucius. They were kind to him. And they seemed happy he was with us. And I remember introducing him to guests of theirs, when they would have their friends over, and everyone was friendly, of course.

"We just did everything together," he went on. "He didn't come to school with me, but he was waiting for me when I got home. He actually used to help me with my 'rithmetic. He wasn't educated, and he wasn't any good at all at English class homework, or writing. In fact, he could just barely ever read, just barely a little. But he had a natural aptitude with numbers and figures. It was the damndest thing really, when you think about it. He just got that stuff. And when I'd work on my 'rithmetic, he'd kind of look along, and when my figuring would start wandering off the right course, damned if he wouldn't say like, 'Massa Benno, I think you might better try it 'dis way.' And he was right. He was always right. Natural aptitude for numbers. Like your people do. Maybe he had some Jew blood in him."

He winked at me. Again, all his stereotypes ran in my favor, and I sensed this kind of statement was probably part of his rascally side, so I let it go. He continued.

"So Lucius learned my mathematics with me right up into college. Even up to the freshman calculus course I took at UGA. He got it all, and better than me." He chuckled.

"What did he do all day, when you were at school?"

"I don't really know. Passed the time. Probably helped with chores around the house. He made my bed, cleaned my bedroom, kept the bathroom I used clean. When I was younger, any toys I was playing with, he'd clean them up. But I'm not sure how he spent all his time. I never really thought about it. Mostly, I reckon he waited for me. Did the same in college. I'd go to classes, and he'd stay in my room. He slept on a palette on the floor in my bedroom. I remember he used to ask if he could use a few shirts I'd already worn that week as a pillow. He'd ball them up at the head of his palette. He slept *soundly*. I could come back to the room all juiced up, roaring drunk, hell, I might trip over him, and he'd sleep right through it. Or if he woke up at all, he might just say 'Night, Massa. Welcome back,' and roll over and go on sleeping. Amazing. Now of course, if I was sick, he'd help me heave it out, you know, hold me steady. And then help me back to bed. Always reliable, always ready for whatever mess I fell into. Damned good slave. Really, he was. I couldn't have asked for better."

Some of these details landed like body blows: sleeping on the floor, "damned good slave." But I wasn't there to argue with an old man; I was there to listen. I had sensed something hanging in the air around Benno, like he had something stored up. Something in his eyes maybe -- a hint of mischief, or truth -- and, as old as he was, even an improbable hint of youth. I have to admit I was glued to the story. "What did the other students think about him?"

"They knew Lucius. They understood why he was there. This was the late forties. The University was all White. Would be 'til 1961 I think. Most students didn't have a slave; I know it was kind of a luxury I had. I lost my parents, but they blessed me with Lucius. So, you know, I was A-OK. But you'd see other slaves around. The dining halls -- all slaves. Serving, making the food, dishes. It was the norm."

Obviously, the University of Georgia campus wasn't run as a slave plantation in the 1940s. But I supposed it could've looked like one to Benno if he'd already made the leap to believing he himself had a slave. "Could Lucius eat with you in the dining halls?"

"Nooooo. No, no. That wasn't allowed. I'd bring him back some food wrapped up in a napkin most times. He liked that. I'd get back, give him the little, you know, makeshift package of food I'd brought. I'd lay down on my bed, and he'd sit on the floor next to me, a couple feet away, and he was so grateful. Loved those little meals. I'm telling you, he was as good as they come. Never a fussy eater. Happy. Full of health. Just great."

"So that was every meal?" I asked.

"Not every meal, no. I'd say it was a pretty regular kind of treat, though. A lot of times, you know, I'd give him a dollar or two so he could go out to the market and fetch some groceries for us. And I'd tell him to be sure to buy himself a Coca-Cola to have for the walk back. He loved Coke. A true Atlantan! Coca-Cola. 'Passport to Refreshment.' That's a slogan I remember. 'Passport to Refreshment.'" He smiled.

"It was like that when we were kids, too. I'd have a few coins, and we'd walk to the store, probably a mile. At that time we lived on West Paces, and we'd walk down to Peachtree to buy a Coke at the general store or the Mobil station. I reckon we did that just about every goddam day." He smiled, and then, "Oh, sorry, Rabbi. I shouldn't take the Big Guy's name in vain."

"Well, maybe not," I responded. "But remember I'm not a rabbi, anyway. So feel free."

"All right then. That's right. I'll feel free. I'll have *at* it! I'll let the good goddams flow like water from the rock!"

"Like milk and honey," I offered.

"Amen, son! Good, giddity goddams flowing like milk and honey! All right. So, son, you following me so far? Am I giving you the sense of how special Lucius was?"

"Yessir, Benno. You absolutely are."

"All right. Alrighty. Good. So when we were kids. Yes. We'd just set out with a dollar or two. This was the 1930s and 40s. Kids walked places all over. Parents didn't give a hoot. We were

42

free to *roam*. And Buckhead then, there were really lovely, gracious mansions, beautiful neighborhoods. But it was residential. You didn't have the big office building skyline like you do now. And there was a lot of forest still. Just woods. You could turn off a street and just disappear for a mile it seemed like. There were empty, wooded acres. Just *disappear*. Lucius and I spent a lot of time in the woods together. We made up different games. Sometimes we'd play cowboys and Indians. I'd play the cowboy, and Lucius was the Indian. Although really I was more like a half cowboy, half militiaman, because cowboys, you know, were more of a western thing. So anyway, I'd count to a hundred and he'd hide and then I'd hunt for him. You could wander for minutes and minutes, and *miles* it felt like. I had read some Indian history books and I knew the names of the Cherokee chiefs who ruled around Georgia. Sometimes I told Lucius he was Chief Black Fox. But usually I called him by the name of Chief Little Turkey, which was a funny name even though Little Turkey was a big deal Chief." Benno was in full conductor mode like when I first saw him. Hands, body, eyes, all moving with the story.

"So we'd range through the woods, with Lucius ahead of me on evasive maneuvers, and I'd be calling out 'I'm on you, you Little

43

Turkey,' or 'Come out of your dark hole, Black Fox.' Like that. It was some kind of fun. It was a mixed woods of pine and hardwoods. I can still smell it. The trees and the ground. It was fresh... and earthy... and ripe. Gawd! It was great." He paused. "Anyway, I won when I tracked him down close enough to pelt him with a clod of dirt or a stick or something. We had a lot of good times playing that game." Benno laughed.

"Lucius didn't mind when you, um, threw dirt or a stick at him?"

He let out a big laugh now, a guffaw, "No! Mind? He loved it! Mordecai, understand we were both filthy from tramping around in the woods already. He didn't care. Hell, sometimes when I won, I'd tell him to roll around in the dirt. Because I won, but also because he *loved* it. He loved being outside. Sometimes we'd camp out in the back yard. I was in the tent, and Lucius would sleep right outside the tent flap. He would be the guard, the sentry. I was the general, and I posted him there, you know, for security. To run off any of my sworn enemies that might attack. He'd sleep out there right on the ground. No sleeping bag. Nothing over his head. If it was cold, I'd give him a blanket. But he liked to sleep right on the ground and look up at the stars. That was Lucius.

44

After I retired to my general's quarters for the night, lots of times I'd hear him talking. He'd talk to the sky, you know. Like to each of the stars *personally*. He'd ask them questions like 'How old is you?' or like 'Can you see me, too?' I'm telling you he was deep. Simple questions. Child's questions. And after all, we were just children. But a deep soul. I remember he'd sometimes talk to the grass, the blades of grass. I peeked out under the tent flap one night, and I remember he was lying on his side talking to the blades of grass the way you'd talk to a person. One of his common discussions with them was about the dew. Did they get cold with the dew. If he was thirsty, he asked if they minded if he drank some of their drops. 'Sho' it's ok?' he'd ask. I mean I had to hold the laughs in. It just tickled me. It was beautiful. And he'd talk to the moon. 'Mistuh Moon,' he called it. 'How is you up there, Mistuh Moon?' And then, 'Oh. Well, my oh my, Mistuh Moon,' and he'd maybe have a quiet laugh. 'That's a good one. You's a funny one.' And then maybe he'd say something like, 'What did da sun say to da moon? No...that's not right, Mistuh Moon. Mistuh Sun said, "wake up!" to da moon.' And then he'd quietly laugh again. 'Gotcha, Mistuh Moon. I gotcha on dat one.'" I could listen to him out there with the moon and the stars and the trees and the grass for a long while before I drifted off. He was at home out there."

Benno got quiet for a moment, and his eyes got watery. It was hard to listen to these memories and not get caught up with him in that memory world; it was a pure place, and filled with affection.

"Anyhow," he continued, "that was what our life was like when I was growing up. A lot of stories, a lot of times like that." He lit up. "Oh, here's another one you'll like. Every year, my mother and father went to Europe for a month in the summer. They went with some of their group. Lucius and I stayed back of course. Parents didn't bring their kids on trips then. And the folks my parents had working in the house, Franklin and Sarah, they stayed back as well. Anyhow, one year my father discovered a men's cologne in Italy called Colonia, by Acqua di Parma. Now realize that back then, cologne hadn't really become a thing for men. In World War II, Old Spice kind of became popular, but this was the 1930s, so it was really a fancy kind of thing. Dad brought back a few bottles, and he became really enamored of it. Well, every now and then, Lucius and I used to sneak up into dad's dressing room and put a little on. Oh, we just cracked ourselves up with that. We knew how fancy we were, all perfumed up like Italian gentlemen. But we also both thought it sort of *stunk*. It was *strong*. And we put too much on. Usually after that we'd go do something outside. Sometimes we'd walk down to the store just to see the looks we got once they smelled us. We knew adults liked that kind of thing, so we figured they were impressed. But again, it was awfully strong for us then. One way or another we'd dirty ourselves up or jump in the creek on the way back home because the smell was too much.

"I actually still wear Colonia. Sometime after college I figured out the proper amount to put on, and I liked it. Funny it's the one thing -- or the biggest thing -- that's always made me feel close to dad. Colonia from Acqua di Parma. Lucius kept wearing it, too. He used to come to work with me at my law office. I let him drive me, and then most of the day he'd wait in the car, though I didn't mind, if it was hot, if he came in and sat in the waiting area. Between the two of us, my little office could smell like the Italian Riviera. Lucius was sure proud to wear that Italian cologne. I think he felt it distinguished him from the other slaves. I was glad I let him do that."

One of the aides came over. "Mr. Benno, we need to get you out for your daily walk."

47

"Oh, thank you, Destiny. You're right." He turned to me, "Mordecai, time for my walk. Need to keep these old bones hoppin'. What say we talk more next week? I'm enjoying this! How about you? Do we have a date?"

"I'll be here if you are. God willing."

"God willing! You said it, son. God willing." He smiled, got up with care and grace as before, and was off.

As I got up to go, I noticed that a gentleman around my age wearing a doctor's coat was sitting by himself on the other side of the dining room making notes. He had noticed me as well and smiled as I was about to leave the dining room and head back to the lobby. I walked out into the hallway, but my curiosity nagged at me, so I turned around, went back in, and introduced myself. This particular doc was a neuropsychiatrist. The Home had a special memory care program which may have explained Benno's placement there. It probably also explained why Benno often didn't seem too different from some of his fellow residents.

"Excuse me, doctor," I said. "My name's Tree Weissman. Do you have a minute?"

"I do. I'm Doctor McBurney," he extended his hand, "Nice to meet you. Please, sit down."

I sat down across from him. "So Doctor, I have kind of an awkward question for you, but-"

"What's the deal with Benno," he interjected. "I'm guessing that's your question, correct?"

"Correct. You got it. I mean, he didn't really have a slave, did he?" I asked.

"Well, as far as we can tell, no. There's no record of a Lucius that we've been able to find. We haven't done an exhaustive investigation, but nothing like that turns up in the usual records. He's old enough for his memory to play tricks on him. And trauma can also play a role; you know his parents died suddenly when he was fairly young. On the other hand, we haven't been able to prove the negative either. I *will* say that when he was growing up, Atlanta was a different place. The assumptions and norms were very different. So I'd say doubtful, but not impossible. When he first got here, we challenged him on it once, lightly, but he wouldn't budge. The other answer to your question is, yes, as far as Benno's concerned, Lucius was real."

We probably chatted there for around five minutes. The doc went on to say that Benno seemed otherwise normal for his age and that there was no specific diagnosis that perfectly fit him. Maybe some version of delirium, but even that didn't quite fit, was too broad. Doctor McBurney was a pleasant man and seemed knowledgeable. There was a lot about the brain that we didn't know, he said. And while this struck me at first as a platitude, I'm quite sure he was correct.

Chapter 3

What a tired world.

The rain won't stop falling.

And what a cranky world. No one knows what to do with their crankiness. You might try drugs, try to shoot the crank in and the cranky out. You might try politics, and let it shoot into your brain the stupidity, the anger, the meanness, the deceit. Cranky, cranky world.

When I was a kid, my parents let me choose my own wallpaper for my room. Probably I was ten. It was the seventies. I chose a pattern that I viewed as happy and cheerful. It was a white background, and on the background were big block letters, primary color words. SO WHAT. WHO CARES. WHY NOT. WAY OUT. GROOVY. FAR OUT. NO WAY. Each "O" was a fully colored circle.

I'd like to be able to greet the world today with these cheery block letters and primary colors, these colored-in circles. It was lost on me that SO WHAT, WHO CARES, and NO WAY were not the most sunshiney phrases. I saw the big shapes and the bright colors. True, in the seventies, SO WHAT and WHO CARES had a certain late flower-child-period élan to them. Even NO WAY, if the accents are right, bespeaks wonder, not opposition. NO *WAY*, to which, now, the proper response might be *WAY*.

I'm looking for the WAY OUT, WHY NOT, FAR OUT, GROOVY America. Boy oh boy, does it seem gone, gone, gone.

I sit by this river. This Chattahoochee. I love rivers. They keep moving. They fill up and they empty out. But it's been a wet spring and summer. Rain most days. And the river collects everything. Dirt and branches and pesticides and dog shit, it all runs off and pours in and floats by. Deflated inner tubes abandoned by drunken river floaters -- shooting the 'Hooch they call it -- wash by or get caught and tangled on low hanging branches and fallen trees. The local non-profit has made great progress over the years, and the river is almost always legally clean, which is to say the measured level of impermissible, toxic crap stays beneath the thresholds. But the rain, the rain, the rain stirs everything up, and my clear green river has run opaque and brown these last two seasons. It rains and the river rises, to near-flood or flood stage, spilling out onto my lawn, twenty, thirty feet past its banks. And when it subsides, it leaves a coat of mud over the grass and bushes and lower tree branches it had covered. And that coat stays until it rains more and washes the stain away. And then if it rains too much, up the river rises, and the cycle repeats.

Still, the river runs. And steady. And sometimes fast. From the southern Appalachians in north Georgia, it runs 434 mostly southwesterly miles, forming the border between Georgia and Alabama for a portion of its course, and joining first with the Flint River as it flows across the Florida-Georgia line, and then the two become one with the Apalachicola River which empties out into the Gulf of Mexico, around an hour and a half southwest of Tallahassee. Apalachicola is famous for its oysters. Oysters are great filter feeders. Each one can filter gallons of water a day, pulling out plankton and other organic debris. They help keep the water clean. But that's way south, way past where I am. I'm part of the system supplying the organic debris.

I have two kayaks. One for me, and one for a friend. When the water is clear and I can see the bottom, I like to drop the kayak in right here at the end of my lawn and go for a paddle. Usually the current is calm, and I can paddle down around a mile and a half where I stop at the Atlanta Water Works facility, turn around, and paddle back up. There's a portage by the Water Works, out and around a five-foot waterfall to the right, but I've never had any interest in going farther. It's around fifteen minutes downstream and twice that back up. It's extremely peaceful. Only once have I encountered anyone else out there. The take-out for the recreational paddlers and floaters is two miles upstream from my house, so no one makes it down to my part of the river unless they know someone in one of the few houses along the banks or they missed the take-out spot and are looking to improvise an exit. When I've brought people out with me, they've all remarked at how quiet and away it is, and hard to imagine it's still Atlanta.

Hard to imagine it's still Atlanta. And easier to imagine it's some other place, some other time. Where it's possible to look away. The world continues to amaze. But the awe and astonishment emanate from dread and disillusion and fear in extremis, as if what used to be north is south and what used to be south is north. Turns out, this north-south switch actually happens every 200,000 years or so; it's called a magnetic pole reversal.

There hasn't been one for 800,000 years now, since the Brunhes-Matuyama reversal, so we're due. Maybe the reversal is nigh, or underway. Doomsday theorists have connected these reversals with the end of the world, although the geologic and fossil evidence runs contrary; the poles have gradually flipped at least hundreds of times over the last three billion years. But it shows you that even the unimaginable comes to pass, and that happy or sad, conscious or ignorant, we survive.

Look away. Let the unknown be the unknown and say peacefully "I don't know." Benno, with his ninety years of life and his departed slave, was more authentically unknowable and unknowably authentic than anyone I'd ever met. And Benno, all ninety years of him, living in an old age home, felt younger to me than anyone I'd spent time with in a long while. He had carried the sweetness of childhood with him all this way. He had kept it alive -- that feeling of openness and adventure, the thickness of thieves, true friendship. Yes, I could feel at times complicit, just for listening, in the darker details of his story, but I still looked forward to seeing him. With Benno, I didn't want to look away.

Chapter 4

Saturday had arrived, and services had ended. I looked across the lobby of the Home, and there was Benno giving me a big smile and an efficient wave.

"So, where did we leave off?" he asked as I shook his hand and took a seat.

"I don't know. You told me a lot. Mostly from growing up."

"Yes. Well, there's a lot to tell. Ninety years, son. Ninety *years*. And with Lucius Cincinnatus Jones for around eighty of them. A *long* time."

"How long ago did he die?" I asked.

"Right before I came here. Or a little before. It's been three years, I think." He paused to verify, "Yes, three years."

"August 16th."

"Yes! That's right. I guess I told you that."

"You did. Did he die of old age?"

Benno caught his breath for a short moment, and then slowly exhaled. It was almost a sigh. He started to lightly tap his hands on his legs as he sat there. "No," he answered. "Not really old age." He shifted in his chair.

"Oh...." I had become nervous of the answer. Benno let out another audible breath.

"You want to know what happened?" he asked. I nodded. "Well, it's not a short story. It'll cost you a chunk of time."

"I've got time."

He leaned forward a little. He held his hands in a prayer gesture, palm to palm, up to his lips. He let out another big breath.

"You've got time, have you? I haven't told this beginning to end since I told the docs before I came here. You sure you want the whole megillah?"

"I'm sure."

"Alrighty, son." He paused again, for a longer moment this time. "Here goes."

And so commenced the story of Benno's last three days together with Lucius, his slave.

"It was summer. Three years ago. 2014. I had long since aged out of the necessity to pretend I had a true job, so most of my time consisted of running a simple errand with Lucius, like the pharmacy or supermarket or something, or more or less lollygaggin' around the house. And oh yes, we'd also go to Capital City Club for lunch, in Brookhaven. Not every day, but a few days a week I'd say. I could eat in the Men's Grille with some of the old crew, or upstairs overlooking the golf course, or, during the summer, it was nice to sit in the downstairs dining room overlooking the pool. Lucius would stay around the car, and I'd bring him a plate or napkin filled with food on the way out."

"Like you did in college."

"Like I did in college. Yes. Anyway, make a long story short, we didn't do a whole hell of a lot. I was, what, eighty-seven. The options, Mordecai, the options had become limited. I joked with Lucius about taking up a kind of daytime residence at The Diamond Club or The Cheetah -- those are strip clubs, you know, titty bars. Burlesques. I don't know what you call them nowadays."

"Strip clubs still works," I offered. "Titty bars, yeah. Burlesques, you don't hear that one really anymore."

"Of course not! Because it has some class to it. Well, in any event, you get the picture. I used to joke with Lucius about that idea. 'Course he was game for anything. We thought about it some. I didn't figure to see anyone I knew there, so that was good. On the other hand, I didn't reckon there were too many octogenarians in those places. Almost nonagenarians, for goodness sake! I remember Lucius said, "Massa Benno, they might likely not come give you any dance for fearin' you die on da spot!' He'd laugh his laugh, and I laughed, and we thought the better of it. So not much going on, son. Not much cooking. As a rule."

"I can see how that would be."

"Not much cooking. So one afternoon, later afternoon, it had cooled off a little, we decided to put the canoe in the river and have a paddle. I told you I lived on the river, right?" he asked.

"You did. Yes. And I'm sorry to interrupt, but where on the river did you live? I actually live on the river myself."

"Really? How about that. It's kind of a tucked away few houses at the end of the Deerfield neighborhood. Off Old Orchard Drive. Where's your place? Probably Columns, or Spalding Drive."

I was stunned. "No, believe it or not, I live on Deerfield Drive."

"You don't say!" he said. "Which house? I was at number 180."

"I'm in 200."

"That's the Royston house," he said. "The red brick."

"I bought it from Mrs. Royston. I painted the brick white, but yes, that's it!" I was amazed. "And just a little while before I moved in, the Thomases moved in to your house, right?" He nodded. "Probably six months before I moved to the neighborhood. Wow."

"That's right, the Thomases. That's who I sold to. Isn't that something."

Benno had lived exactly two doors south, or downstream, from me. It was hard to believe. People still referred to his former home as "the Johnson house" even though the Thomases had lived there three years already, just as they still referred to my house as the Royston house. As in, "Sally, you've met Tree, right? He moved into the Royston house." And Sally, who would be a neighbor I hadn't met, would say "Ohhhh. Yes. Nice to meet you. How long has it been? Around six months, I guess?" even if it had been much longer. It's the way of neighborhoods; oftentimes, it only becomes your house once you've moved out. In retrospect, I had heard the

Thomas house referred to as the Johnson house, but the name was so common, it didn't really make a mark with me, and even when Benno mentioned he lived on the river, nothing registered. Benno's house was the last house at the downstream end of our street, hard up against the large Arnaud property, which old man Arnaud had once let people stroll across to get to the polo fields beyond it, but which was now gated and fenced off.

There are ten houses along the river at the end of Deerfield Drive where Benno once lived and I still do. It's an interesting bit of topography. We have the river on one side; a wooded swamp on the other side; and at the south or downstream end of the street, there's the fenced off Arnaud property which is ten or fifteen mostly open acres; and then beyond that is the Atlanta Polo Club, another wide open tract, which is on land owned by a gentleman named Otto Schiffer, who also owns the land and home on the other side of the polo field. Schiffer grew up in Atlanta; his parents had moved here between the World Wars. In Germany, his family had built up a large auto parts manufacturing firm. The Schiffer business started in the early 1900s, became large and then larger during World War II, kept growing and was ultimately purchased by one of the large post-war German conglomerates. Otto Schiffer owned a large piece of land, loved horses and polo, and gave a great swath of his property to found the Atlanta Polo Club. He kept a low profile, but he was regarded as an upright, civic-minded man.

"Well, good then. You'll be able to picture everything exactly," Benno continued. "What a small world." He said this as a statement of fact, not wonder, whereas I was by this point pretty close to slack-jawed at the coincidence.

"So we put the canoe in the river and put ourselves in the canoe. We each had on a pair of our old man trunks and aqua socks. I tell you what, son -- I don't think they would've put us on a fashion runway. But we were ready."

"Style comes from within," I noted. I'd come up with that one in exchanges with my daughters to defend my own wardrobe choices and minimize the importance of theirs. Shockingly, they were never fully convinced.

"Quite right, Mordecai! Quite right! I'm making mental note of that little nugget. Well, so there we were, looking as we did. We'd gone out so many times, countless times over the years, but in your late eighties, like we were, it becomes a delicate operation. Well, you must know -- walking down that bank carrying a boat takes some care. So we would watch our steps, kind of amble or shamble on down, and drop her in. I'd get in first, and I'd sit in front. Lucius would hold the canoe steady for me. Then I'd do my best to moor us to something with my arm or paddle as he hopped in. For an old man, Lucius was still strong and balanced. Then we pushed off and headed downstream.

"It hadn't rained too much recently, so the water was that clear green it gets, and the current was easy. We couldn't head downstream of the house unless we knew we could get back upstream, so we really needed a light current that we could paddle through coming back up. But the way it was that day was good when we got started. We just kinda floated downstream nice and easy, enjoying it. There's no one out there, and you can just pull your paddle up and drift along and listen. If there was a little breeze, you could hear it gentle on the water. And you could just sit there and watch the leaves on the tops of trees thrash around with the heavier breeze, and watch the branches and boughs up top sway. It's like you're in a different weather system on the river. Almost still. And up at the top, say, third of the trees, it can look like a storm's blowing through. You know what I mean?"

"I do. I've been there."

"Well, it's something. So Lucius and I were just drifting around in a generally downstream direction. The big old turtles were out sunning themselves on the branches of dead trees sticking up over the surface. Eastern River Cooters. They live like forty, fifty years, you know. The Eastern Box Turtles that you might see by the swamp now and then, they can live a hundred years!"

"I didn't know that."

"Well, they can. Now, the Cooters, they're Nervous Nellies. You just can't get up too close to them. I don't know what they think we want to do with them, catch them maybe they think. Though I don't know anyone who hunts turtles. Evolutionary wiring, I suppose. They fall off those logs into the river before you can get within twenty-five feet of them usually.

"So Lucius and I are moving along. Float downstream a little, paddle across side to side to see what we see. Not saying much of anything. It was a nice, quiet, peaceful afternoon, probably around five-thirty or six. Easy current, almost slack sometimes. Light, light wind. Few hours of daylight to play with, and we had no intention of being out a few hours. *Maybe* an hour. Down most of the way to the Water Works then back up. SOP, you know. Standard operating procedures."

"Right," I said.

"Right. Lovely day. Lovely." He had one of his far away pauses. I let it continue. Breathing in, breathing out. Breathing in, breathing out. Probably twenty seconds passed. "...Lovely." He came back into what I'd call a soft focus. "We were just out there. Paddling."

He went into a pause again, and I interjected "So what happened then?"

"What happened then? The river started moving on us. It started moving fast just like that," he snapped, "and we got caught up in it."

This was a long time theoretical fear of mine. At any point, for reasons unclear to the denizens such as we living downstream, a decision could be made by the Army Corps of Engineers to release more than the usual quantity of water out of Lake Lanier and over the Buford Dam. This in turn could cause Georgia Power to release extra water over the Morgan Falls Dam which it operates further downstream and closer to us. In the most extreme case, which occurred in the Fall of 2009 at the end of a particularly rainy fortnight, these releases would cause catastrophic flooding downstream. I didn't own my house yet in 2009, but it was flooded four feet deep, as was every other house on our street. The river rose then to a level of twenty-nine feet. Around four or five feet is the norm. It overflowed the banks at around ten feet, covered my house's eighty-yard-long back yard at probably sixteen or seventeen feet, came up the raised embankment upon which my house is built and overflowed that at around twenty-three feet, and kept rising another six feet completely flooding the first floor of my house, "the Johnson house," and every other house at our river-hugging end of the neighborhood. All the houses were built on raised plots like mine, but none were raised on stilts or pillars as no such flood had previously occurred. After the storm, some neighbors chose to use a portion of their insurance money to raise their houses, but most houses, including mine and Benno's old house, remain on the ground, the owners implicitly betting against another five-hundred-year flood during their habitation in the neighborhood.

This was an extreme case. And people blamed the Army Corp of Engineers and Georgia Power for not better planning, better staging their releases from their respective dams -- for not giving due consideration to the residences along the river downstream. There were hearings, the buck was passed back and forth, and most people who live here concluded there was some element of negligence by someone that caused the damage to our homes. They say that while the flooding built at a steady pace up to around eighteen or nineteen feet, the river rose its final ten feet suddenly, in not much more than an hour, which many people link to ill-conceived and unnecessary dam releases. This may have been the case. It may also be the case that we like telling ourselves this, and telling ourselves that the Corps of Engineers and Georgia Power have been sufficiently chastised, in order to comfort ourselves that our homes won't flood again, that nature unbounded won't do us in by itself, that the humans in control are now on notice.

Even well short of this extreme case, there are routine releases from each dam, and even a modest variation from the routine could have an impact on two old men in a canoe.

"Was there a release from the dams?" I asked.

"Well, there sure shot must have been. Because we went from slack tide to riding the rapids in no time flat. I remember I said something like 'Well, what the hell,' and Lucius said, 'Oh, Massa Benno. This ain't no good. This ain't no good at all!'"

"How far downstream were you when it picked up?"

"Not so far. Between the Arnaud property and the polo fields. We were on our side of the river, so first thing we tried was to angle ourselves over to that little stream between the polo fields and the Schiffer property and try to get hung up in there and then climb up to the polo fields. I was paddling as hard as I could on the left, and Lucius was trying to turn us with a steady braking on the right. We got to a paddle's length away, and Lucius stood up and reached for a branch. I was worried he was going to fall in because he wasn't a strong swimmer. But his balance was good as always, and he actually grabbed onto a branch. We each let out a kind of 'hey, hey!' But the downstream current was too strong, and there was current coming into the river from that little stream as well, and it twisted us and pushed us away. He fell and landed three-quarters out of the boat, but the current actually somehow popped him up so he could plant himself back in again.

"I pivoted around on my seat and said to him 'Lucius, you okay?' He looked back at me. He was half soaked and breathing heavy. And I'll never forget, he kind of caught his breath, and wiped his hand over his face.

"'Massa Benno,' he said, 'I think we's about to enjoy this ride.'

"'Enjoy this ride?!' I said. And then we both just cracked up laughing. What the hell were we even doing out there! Two old guys going ten miles an hour downstream and can't stop. I mean, what in the world!" He snorted at himself. One leg was tapping; his eyes were big then small with expression; he was working his arms and hands as he spoke. Like a kid, he looked like a ninety-year-old kid.

"You laughed," I said.

And he laughed again. "Seemed like the natural response to the situation, Mordecai. The most reasonable response. It still breaks me up, tickles me to think of it. Lucius with those big white eyes, 'I think we's about to enjoy this ride, Massa Benno.' He could sum it up.

"So we kept on floating downstream. It was like being a part of something pretty darn dreadful that was happening pretty quickly but not so quickly that you didn't have time to appreciate how dreadful it actually was. We were going about as fast as I might have gone when I was younger at a good steady downstream paddle. But of course we weren't paddling; we were just being carried by the current. We went by Schiffer's house, past that sculpture of a pack of hunting dogs that he has out by the riverside.

We went by and had time to notice the couple of nice houses on the left side, and then got up to the industrial use area on our side of the river as we were coming up on the water intake and treatment facilities. We knew what was waiting for us. We were going to end up going over one of those little waterfalls that the buoys warn you against. And even if we managed to steer ourselves to the waterfall on the right, we knew we weren't going to be able to get over and carry the canoe around. Actually, Lucius asked if he oughta try to steer us over in that direction, but because I knew that even if we made it over to the portage we were going to continue downstream, I just decided, with the water running high, you know, let's shoot this rapid. Now, you could say that was a crazy decision, and you'd be right. I know that. But having lived to tell the tale, I can tell you it was the hot diggity doggest, most crazy-ass thing me and Lucius had ever done. Or certainly had ever done in a good many decades. We came up on that little waterfall, and I said to Lucius, 'Paddle strong and true, my boy. Strong and true!' And he said, 'Yessuh, Massa Benno! Yessuh!!!' The bow with me in it surged out over the falls, we plunged down five feet, and shot out of that little watery maelstrom of death like natural born champions, Mordecai! Natural born champions!"

The river was flowing, Benno was flowing, and I was riding right along with him.

"Amazing," I said. "I've seen videos on the internet of a couple people doing that, but that's young, daredevil types."

"Exactly! Exactly as you say, Mordecai. I'm telling you, it was flat-out stupid that we did it, but once we'd done it, we let out the biggest war whoop that two old sets of lungs could whoop up. I looked back at Lucius. He was soaked, and now I was soaked, too. And we just looked at each other and started back laughing, laughing, laughing.

"What an experience. So. We got ourselves back together, took stock of where we were, and continued on downstream. The water was slowing down, but we both knew we weren't going to be able to paddle back, and neither of us had been downstream this far before. So we decided, well, let's keep on down the ol' Hooch and see what we see. Like I said, we were wet. But fortunately it was a warm enough evening, and there was a nice, little, warm breeze from our movement along the river, so that we didn't get cold and even started to dry off a bit.

"Now that stretch of the river, I don't know if you've ever looked at a map, but it is entirely bordered by industrial firms of one sort or another. The city's water treatment facilities take up a whole lot of space, and then you just have a lot warehouses. Of course, you can't see everything from the river. Depends on how steep the bank is right where you are. But you don't see any houses. And what you hear tends to be the whirring of machines of one sort or another. So we just paddled along and took it in. As I think back, even though it was a river and we were in a canoe and there's nothing wrong with that, it still felt almost like we were breaking in somewhere. We just knew we were somewhere doing something that people hadn't much done and really weren't supposed to do if they had any sense. That's a good feeling, feeling like you're doing something wrong and knowing that you're not. It's like being a legal outlaw if you know what I mean."

"I do." And I did. I hadn't thought about it in those terms or put it in those words to myself, but I knew exactly what he meant. I could get that feeling just living in the South, just from the very fact that I lived here but wasn't from here. It was a strange thing to live a life I knew to be totally respectable and yet at the same time feel vaguely suspect. It could feel that way being Jewish sometimes as well. That's a bigger statement than Benno's, but I knew the feeling.

"So we continued on. Paddling. Taking in the scenery. Commenting to each other upon the more particularly pungent industrial aroma zones we would float through. And I remember so clearly, like I can hear it right now, Lucius started singing a song we used to sing together on our adventures when we were kids. I don't think he or I had sung it or probably thought about it for sixty or seventy years. And he just started in like it was yesterday in his rich ol' voice. He sang a verse, then I did, then we'd do the choruses together. Just like it was yesterday." And Benno began to sing.

Way down upon the Swanee River,

Far, far away

That's where my heart is turning ever

That's where the old folks stay

All up and down the whole creation,

Sadly I roam

Still longing for the old plantation

And for the old folks at home

All the world is sad and dreary everywhere I roam

Oh darkies, how my heart grows weary

Far from the old folks at home

All 'round the little farm I wandered,

When I was young

Then many happy days I squandered,

Many the songs I sung

When I was playing with my brother,

Happy was I

Oh, take me to my kind old mother,

There let me live and die

All the world is sad and dreary everywhere I roam

Oh darkies, how my heart grows weary

Far from the old folks at home

One little hut among the bushes,

One that I love

Still sadly to my mem'ry rushes,

No matter where I rove

When shall I see the bees a humming,

All 'round the comb

When shall I hear the banjo strumming,

Down by my good old home

All the world is sad and dreary everywhere I roam

Oh darkies, how my heart grows weary

Far from the old folks at home

He sang the whole song. He was ninety years old, so he was forgivably flat on the notes, but the tone of his voice was lovely and of good timbre. By his conductor's gestures he had told me when Lucius was singing, when he took his verse, and when they sang the choruses together.

"You know -- now I didn't know this when I was a kid, when Lucius and I used to sing that together out on our expeditions -- but that's a song about a slave, longing to be back with his family, back on the 'old plantation.' That's what that line's about. I was always glad that Lucius had already lost his family when he came to me.

You know? That I didn't break him apart from his mommy and daddy."

"Mordecai his daddy," I said, again feeling somehow complicit in his story, as though my listening to it, my absorption in it, was making it more real.

"That's right. His daddy Mordecai. We hadn't sung that song in a long time. A long, long time. And we just drifted along. It was starting to get darker. The sky was still blue, but the sun was gone behind the trees up on the banks of the river. You know how you're lower when you're on the river. Lower down. If I'd been on my front yard, I probably could still see the sun, but down on the river, it was just the leftover light. Funny how songs stay in your head and just come back on you sometimes. We both remembered all the words. Just like the old times. It was peaceful out there."

He paused briefly.

"Well, I decided as lovely as ol' Swanee River was, it was a bit on the sad side. So I started in on one a little brighter. Another one of our old walking songs. 'The Sunny Side of the Street.' You know that one, Mordecai. 'Grab your coat and get your hat....'"

"Yes, indeed" I responded. "Leave your worries on the doorstep...."

"That's the one," he said. For this one it seemed, from Benno's conducting, that Lucius fell in with him almost right away, and they sang it together.

"We loved that one. Happy marching music, you know what I mean? Jolly. Jolliness is an underrated trait, Mordecai. We could all use some more jolly. When we finished singing, Lucius, just like he used to, he said 'Rockafella', Massa Benno. Imagine that. Rich as Rockafella'! My oh my.' And he laughed. He loved that line. I think he enjoyed saying Rockafella'. It's a fun word to say. It's pleasing out of the mouth. Try it, son."

I tried it. He was right. "It *is* pleasing."

"It *is* pleasing! Damn right, it is! Makes you feel kind of happy and rich and, I don't know, *hip*, all at the same time! Lucius loved it. He'd just repeat it. 'Rockafella', rich as Rockafella', and he'd laugh or let out a kinda whistle. Like whoo-wee. Makes me happy remembering.

"So it was getting dark, but we were feeling pretty good on the river, good spirits, still floating downstream through that kind of industrial no-man's land. Still floating downstream. All this time, by the way -- and you'll know what I mean -- one of those beautiful, really elegant, blue herons we have was flying along with us, near us, flying on ahead and perching on a fallen tree, waiting for us to catch up, and then flying on a bit farther. Such graceful birds. Felt like she was listening to us sing. It was a comfort. That kind of beauty moving with us.

"So the heron and us, we're moving downstream. And like it is when you get to singing with someone, I already had thought of the *next* song while we were still singing the last one. Another one that Lucius and I used to have almost like a routine to. Where he'd chime in after certain lines, like color commentary, or, I don't know..."

"Like call and response," I interjected.

"Call and response, Mordecai! Yes, just as you say. Showing your religious bent there. Like call and response. Something like that. So I started in to singing 'Sit down you're rocking the boat.' You know that one, Mordecai?"

"Guys and Dolls. I sure do. And, of course, a great boat song. Appropriate for the setting."

"Yes it was. Well, we laid in to that one then. I'd get to the line, "And I hollered 'someone fade me,' and Lucius would come back with 'Fade me!' When I said, 'The people all said sit down,' Lucius would shout out 'Sit down!' Like that. When I said the line about having a bottle in my fist, he'd say something like 'Oh my, Massa Benno!' We had a good time. We finished that one, and we laughed and laughed. And then, you know that first line, Mordecai, about being on the boat to heaven?"

I told him I did.

"Well, this was another good one. We'd finished singing the song and were just drifting along. Peaceful as far as I was concerned. Probably a couple minutes passed. And Lucius, he says to me, 'You reckon we on 'dat boat now, Massa Benno?'

"What boat, Lucius?

'Well, 'dat boat to heaven, Massa Benno.'

"I laughed and told him no, but I knew where he was coming from with that one. Both of us old and floating down the river. I don't believe I ever taught Lucius any Norse mythology, but now that he mentioned it, it wasn't hard for me to imagine us floating aflame like a Viking funeral, all the way down to Apalachicola or as far as we got before they found us. But it didn't get me down. I knew we'd find shore somewhere before we found heaven, even if we just washed up. Heaven could wait, you know what I'm saying, Mordecai?"

"I know what you're saying."

"So, right around then, with visions of Viking funeral ships still in my head, Lucius and I notice on the right side of the river, some kind of lit-up, twisted metal surrealist fantasy. And noise. Like the noise of a thousand, *ten* thousand people. From the river, we could only see the top of these wild structures. So I say to Lucius, 'What in God's name is that, boy?' And he says back, 'Massa Benno, if it ain't heaven, I'm afraid of what else it might be.' I took that thought under advisement for a moment, gathered my senses, gained my bearings, and then I saw it. I figured it out. 'Well, son of a gun, Lucius! We're at the amusement park!' 'Amusement park?' he says, and I say 'Yes! The Six Flags Amusement Park! Six Flags over Georgia!'"

Again, Benno was right on. He would have come upon Six Flags just as he said.

"Well, the current was slow enough now for us to angle over to the shore. In fact, it had been slow enough for quite some time, but there wasn't any clear reason to go to shore at any of the other spots further back upstream if all we were going to find was a fence and a factory. This, on the other hand, was a bona fide attraction. We found a piece of shore that looked good and paddled to it. Lucius hopped out of the canoe and pulled us through the knee-deep water and Chattahoochee River mud to a spot where I could also get out, and without a hospitalization event occurring. Still, it was tricky and awkward making the transition because, as you know, you're gonna sink into that river mud pretty deep and when you step up out of it, it's a suction creating event. So it's messy and awkward and I had to be careful.

"Anyway, we got out of the boat and on up a gentle sloping portion of river bank and stood there together for a minute and beheld. I had never been to Six Flags. I was aware of it from reading the newspaper and seeing the television ads, but I'd never been there. And Lucius only knew what a modern amusement park was from seeing those same TV ads. He had never set foot in an amusement park or, for that matter, gone to any carnival or fair of any size. I used to go to some when I was younger, but coloreds oftentimes weren't allowed in, and so Lucius would have to either stay home or if he drove with me, stay in the car or out in the parking lot. So he hadn't really encountered anything of this scale before, and it was just awesome to him. And, to be honest, it was awesome to me as well. I mean, have you been? The crowds! And these roller-coasters! In shapes you can't imagine. Goodness!"

I nodded in agreement, and he went on.

"The first thing we encountered was a gigantic swimming pool that had some kind of action connected to it such that it looked like an ocean coming ashore. A light blue clear ocean. Every so often bigger waves would kick up towards one end of the pool and the people would have a *big 'ol* time, screaming and enjoying the up-and-down of those waves. And along each side of the pool there were people and chairs and recliners and even cabanas as though they were actually at a beach. Probably four hundred people were crowded around this piece of magic water in a state of wonderful self-delusion. The magic water spooked Lucius a bit. He struggled to even really ask me what was going on there. But I put him at ease with my best explanation which was of necessity a lay person-friendly explanation as I lacked entirely the engineering background to describe exactly what *was* really happening and why.

"We walked on towards the entrance of this exhibit or ride or whatever you would call it. Attraction, I guess. And there was a shower available that little kids were using before getting into the pool. We used it to rinse the mud off of our lower legs so we wouldn't look quite as ridiculous as we otherwise would. Or perhaps two old men in aqua socks walking around the amusement park were going to look ridiculous either way. At least with the mud washed off we didn't look like swamp creatures or extras from some zombie ride.

"We started moving over towards this pool contraption. Of course, of the children and adults playing around in the water, there were both Whites and coloreds and about every shading in between. Everything from Mexico to Asia no doubt. We stopped probably fifteen feet from one side of the pool. Like I said, it was that beautiful time of the evening.

"'Look at all the different colors,'" Lucius said. His manner of speaking was usually upbeat, even joyful, but he said this in a kind of dreaminess.

"'Yes, Lucius my boy. A veritable rainbow of children in wet and wild frolic. Quite something to behold, wouldn't you say'?

"'Yes, Massa Benno. Sump'n to behold.'

"It was then I realized that we had never been in a swimming pool together, Lucius and I. It was a realization that kind of snuck up on me and took a hold. We had a pool when I was a child, but it was understood that Lucius was not to go in. Over most of the rest of my life I didn't have a pool, and if I used one it was at the club and of course Lucius would not be using that pool either. We had swum or splashed together growing up so many times in a stream or pond or even a puddle. But it was something to think about that we'd never played together in a pool growing up like all these children here were doing.

"I took his hand. 'What do you say you and I dangle our feet in for a minute before they close down for the day?'

"He didn't say anything, but we walked together hand in hand to the edge of the pool, sat down, and hung are feet down into the water. And there we sat, just sat there for a few minutes looking out over everyone else in the pool through the light of the darkening sky. I remember watching our four calves moving out and back, out and back, slow and easy on the old hinges of our four old knees, and thinking to myself 'There are my legs and there are Lucius's legs in this pool.'"

"Did that alarm you?" I broke in.

"No. No, no. It didn't alarm me," he responded easily. "I just thought to myself, 'Look at this. I haven't seen this before.' It was such a little thing, a *simple* thing, but it struck me. It was a lovely evening, and we just sat there for a few minutes taking it in.

"By and by, we got up and exited the magic water attraction which, turned out, went by the name of Paradise Island.

"'That was nice,' Lucius said.

"And I said 'Yes, it was. What say we wander a bit. See what we see.'

"'Yessuh. I'll see what I see and you see what you see, Massa Benno.'

"'That's a deal,' I said. And off we wandered further into the park.

"People, you could see, were starting to pack up and leave. But there was still a fair amount of action going on. Kids were rushing to get in their last rides on their favorite attractions. We walked out of Paradise Island, and the first two things we saw were two other attractions. One was called Hurricane Harbor, and the other was called Superman: Ultimate Flight. Hurricane Harbor looked kind of similar to where we had just been at Paradise Island. There were people floating around in a large pool. There must have been some kind of hurricane theme to the decor or to the pool that I didn't immediately decipher, but it looked pretty similar. The Superman ride, on the other hand, was a true state-of-the-art looking roller coaster. Now, when I was a kid I had been on some old rickety wooden numbers, but nothing like this. We watched as it swooped through its loops, down and up and around and down again and sideways and up and down and upside down and down and up again, on and on. Lucius was beyond disbelief. The riders would scream as they would go into a plunge and then out of the plunge and into another death-defying aerial maneuver.

"'Dey do sump'n wrong, Massa Benno, or is dey enjoyin' it?' Lucius asked.

"'They're enjoying themselves, Lucius. At least after the manner that you enjoy yourself while you're doing something that's a little crazy and dangerous, but that's probably going to turn out okay. At least nine and a half times out of ten anyway.'

"'Nine and a half times, it's okay?' Lucius asked.

"'I reckon. Probably even ninety nine out of a hundred,' I told him.

"'Well, can we try it then, Massa Benno?' he asked me.

"'Can we try it?!!' I said. 'Have you lost your mind, boy? You hear those people screaming, don't you?'

"And he says, 'I hear them. I hear them, Massa Benno. And I'd like to try that ride!'

"He had become loud with his excitement. I had never been one to enjoy roller coasters even in my youth. But I figured, heck, it wasn't likely that I'd be at an amusement park ever again. Yes, we had stumbled upon it, but I didn't suppose that it was going to become a new regular destination for us. And if ol' Lucius was so hepped up about it, well, why not.

"'Okay,' I said. And my oh my, you'd think Christmas had come in the middle of August for Lucius. Whoopin' it up like a child, and here he was -- and here I was -- going on ninety years old. But boy was he excited. I got a kick out of that, I gotta tell you. Mind you, it was a short bout of whoopin' because at his age he couldn't sustain too many consecutive whoops before his energy waned, and he still needed to have energy left for the ride that was *causing* all that whoopin' in the first place. But it was a window into youth that he was climbing through, and I guess he was pulling me on through it with him, against my better judgement I must say.

"We got in line. It was moving pretty quick, end of the day as it was. But every time we had to stop and wait, Lucius would get more anxious with excitement. Every time we'd hear that crazy chorus of screams, he'd get more hepped up, working his hands together, not keeping his feet still for even a second. When we got to the front of the line, we shuffled on in. Actually, I shuffled; Lucius was closer to a hop. We got into the kind of, well, I don't know what you'd call it. The seats? I guess the seats, of this flight contraption. There were four across. Fortunately, we got one with just the two of us, but I can tell you there were some stares of concernment as we made our way in and got locked down in our harnesses.

"And then. Well, then the ride began. I don't know exactly how to describe it for you, Mordecai. If you haven't done it. You haven't done it, have you, son?"

"No, sir, I haven't" I replied.

"Well, if that's what it's like to be Superman, he can have it. He can just go on saving the world, conquering the bad guys, the whole shebang. Because it was the most miserable -- that ride, that torture chamber -- was the most miserable two minutes of my life. Honestly, Mordecai, leaving aside all the more predictable reactions, like terror and nausea, what can I tell you? I honestly thought, I was convinced, that my bones were gonna break. And listen, I don't just mean like breaking my arm or leg. I mean like my whole skeleton was just gonna give up and crumble down inside of me. And my organs. I couldn't tell you which ones it was, but it was like my kidney or pancreas or something was moving to the other side of my body and back. Just smashing and squeezing around in there, all over the place. Really. Like my organs were relocating. Absolutely terrible. Never do that again."

"I'll make note," I said.

"You do that. You do that, Mordecai! Make note! Not worth it in the least. But listen to this. The ride ends. I sit there. I don't think I could scream during the ride at all for all the moaning, weak moaning I was doing. So we're sitting there as we get unlatched from the harnesses. I'm still moaning. Sitting there, bent over, in full moan. I manage to look over at Lucius, and what do you think I see? Tears. I see tears, just streaming down his old black face. And I ask him, 'You all right, Lucius? You okay, boy?' And he turns to me, and I see that, yes, he's crying, like almost silently crying. But he's smiling! Smiling, too!

"'Wudn't dat sump'n?' he managed. And then he started crying some more, but still smiling, too.

"'Are you smiling or crying, Lucius?' I asked in a moan, trying not to turn my head too much lest I stir up my nausea.

"'Oh,' he said. 'How 'bout dat, Massa Benno. I didn't even notice I was cryin'. Wudn't dat sump'n! I was pretty sure I was Superman for a second. Superman his own self! What a ride!'

"'What a ride,' I moaned. 'C'mon. Let's get away from this thing before it goes again.' He followed me off. But my goodness! About ninety years old though he was, he would've rode that death trap again if he could've. Unreal. Absolutely unreal. Thought he was Superman! Hmmph!

"So I ushered him away from his new pal Superman, and we joined the flow of folks moving towards the exit. I'd decided we'd just leave the canoe where it was and deal with it later if it occurred to me. It was an old canoe anyways, and beaten up. Lucius's seat wasn't really even a seat anymore. You'd sit on it, and it was a push whether it was more pain or comfort. The kinda bamboo weave had come undone, so sharp pieces stuck up at inconvenient angles. We just left it there and headed out with the people. The People, Mordecai! The Great Unwashed! It was truly something to behold. The Blacks and Browns and Yellows and of course the Whites, and every admixture you could imagine. And fat! Not everyone, but a lot of fat people, with no problem at all flaunting it like they're sumo wrestlers or something and proud to be so! Look, it ain't pretty. But I tell you what -- there is a kind of messed up, oh, I don't know, honky tonk beauty to it. And of course, like I said, I can't say either Lucius or I stood out from the crowd as paragons of fashion or form, right? I mean we were just in there with them. In with the flow. Like the river after a storm. Debris. Just lovely human debris.

He was flowing, conducting, lively.

"So we floated along with the crowd. Actually, don't know that you would say I was floating if you saw me. Or if I was, I was barely afloat. That ride took the starch out of me. That's for sure. Lucius, on the other hand, was *absolutely* floating, face all aglow, almost levitating along. Man, if I was barely afloat, just hanging on to a piece of driftwood, he was a veritable hovercraft, riding high. Well, good for him. I was happy for him. Glad he liked it. But we sure-shot weren't coming back, that much I knew. Good grief. I wasn't going to tell Lucius that right then; I was feeling miserable, not mean. But my boy Lucius had flown like the mechanical Superman for the first and last time.

"We left the park and turned right as we exited the gate heading back in a generally upstream direction. We walked along at our typical slow but steady pace, a little slower than usual at first as I was still recovering from the organ rearrangement that had occurred on that infernal ride. But by-and-by, I came to feeling like my regular self, and we kept moving on in that upstream direction. As I've described to you, Mordecai, and as you *know*, it's an industrial sort of zone there. So after-hours and in the evening the only action going on is the ins and outs of cars at the factories that have three shifts. And there were quite a few of those. We had a couple cars pull over and ask us if we needed help, but I guess even in that bedraggled looking outfit, I retained enough of my innate dignity to convince these Good Samaritans that we were okay and just heading to our car a little bit on ahead. So we kept walking.

"By this time, it had become full-on dark. Lucius, of course, wasn't going to ask what my plan was for the evening. That wasn't his place. But I knew that he must be wondering, and in fact, as we walked on in the dark I was wondering the same thing myself. But soon we came upon an empty lot. It was connected to a factory that appeared to be more of a relic than a going concern. Windows here and there were shattered, there was some obscure graffiti, and weeds grew up through cracks in the pavement of the parking lot. While that doesn't sound particularly welcoming, it was empty, and it looked like it would remain empty, so I told Lucius let's stop in here.

"'Yessuh, Massa Benno.' He might have been skeptical of the evening's plans and these particular accommodations, but all he said was, 'It's lookin' to be a beautiful evenin'. I had to agree because it was.

"It had been a very long time since we had set up camp anywhere, though we camped out many times when we were kids. Sometimes we camped out at night. Sometimes we pretended to camp out during the day. It was a building block piece of our young adventurer lifestyle. Camping out! That was something we knew how to do. The thinking about it, talking about it, planning about it in advance. And the setting up and doing of it. And the breaking down of the camp, packing up and moving on afterwards. Foundations of our childhood, Mordecai, *rituals*, that's what these were. So we knew what to do. The only problem was we didn't have anything to do any of it *with*. It was just us in our trunks and our aqua socks and that's it.

"So I said, 'Why don't we collect some of these weeds and see if we've got enough for a couple of small pillows, or at least something to keep our heads off the pavement.' Lucius thought it was a good idea, so he and I went about gathering up some weeds. It was stoop work and not easy at our age and after a long day, but we gathered up what we could, got some bug bites to show for it, and sat down.

"'Looks to me like only enough here to really do one of us any good,' I said. 'How about you can use the weeds, Lucius, and I've got another idea. I'll use our shoes instead for my pillow.'

"'That sound like a good idea, Massa Benno' he answered.

"So that's what we did. His pillow of weeds, my pillow of aqua socks, and we found a more sheltered part of the lot near a tree off to one side and bedded down. I remember that even though the aqua socks were actually not a bad pillow, they smelled of river mud, and that smell was mixed in with a vague condiment odor that must have glommed on in the park. It was mildly nauseating. But, on the other hand, we were lying down, with something under our heads, and like Lucius had said, it *was* a lovely night.

"I started in to humming 'Down in the Valley,' one of our favorite old songs. Some songs are nighttime songs, Mordecai. Some songs are daytime, sunshiney songs, and some are for the nighttime. 'Down in the Valley' -- now that's a nighttime song. And Lucius hummed along with me. And we hummed it over and over, over and over, until I drifted off.

"I had a dream that night that I still remember. I dreamed that it was night and a full moon, and Lucius and I were running

94

across the Arnaud property. We had just leapt over the gate and were running across those acres, through the grove of trees, out into the open, running like young men or even boys, really. Now, it was clear we weren't boys. It was still our own current day bodies, each one with four score and ten worth of mileage. But at the same time it was like we were young. Our bodies -- this body, Mordecai -- was working like it was a boy's. It felt wonderful. We were running on the grass. Bare footed. And I hesitate to share this part, son, and don't try too hard to picture it, but we were naked, me and Lucius. Yes, we were. It makes me chuckle. Me and Lucius running young and naked over Arnaud's forbidden property on a full-moon-lit night. Crazy goddam thing, I know. And it was like we were singing, or laughing. There wasn't sound, but I could tell even so. It had the feeling. We ran and ran and didn't get tired and after a few hundred yards, we noticed that probably eight or nine deer had joined us. All bucks. You usually don't see the bucks much. They hide out. But it was all bucks. I'd say a few of them were eight-pointers, glorious, running right along with us. And it was like we were talking to each other. Not human talking, but some kind of talking, some kind of communicating. And we ran along like that for another couple hundred yards, speeding onward and onward, our strides covering twenty feet at a time, zigging, zagging with the herd. Bounding over the grass. I'll never forget it."

He lingered in that reverie. And I watched him linger. He looked sad and happy and most of all young. Just lingering in that moment, that dream. "That's a beautiful dream," I said to him.

He looked at me with moist eyes and replied, "Yes, it was. And like all dreams it ended. In this case quite suddenly. Lucius nudged me and told me to 'Wake up Massa Benno. Wake up,' he said. One of the old gates to the lot was scraping against the pavement as a man was pushing it open. A number of cars and pickup trucks started coming in. If I had to guess, I'd say there were thirty or forty vehicles all told. We could see them from our sheltered spot as they drove in. Most of the cars and trucks looked on the older side. There were a few motorcycles as well. They all headed over, fortunate for us, to the opposite side of the lot. Diagonally opposite. I would say they were probably a hundred yards away, about a football field's distance.

"When they got out of their cars, we could hear them starting to exchange greetings with each other. These were hardcore crackers, judging by the accents and the general redneck tone of their exchanges. A lot of big laughs and back slaps and 'hell yeahs' and the like were flying around. Now I know, Mordecai, that we're in the South. But you know, you can tell the difference between that kind of Southerner and you or me. First of all, from where we sat, it didn't look or sound like a crowd that included people who had moved to Atlanta to work for Home Depot or Turner. Right? You know what I mean? Beyond that, well, it was just a crude looking and sounding group of fellas. At the same time, it occurred to me that maybe one of these men could give us a ride back home, which we still needed. We wondered what they were up to. Lucius and I looked at each other, and without saying anything to each other, we knew we were on the same wavelength. A little discretion was called for, and we should just hang back for a minute, wait and see what might transpire. It was a sketchy looking scene, Mordecai. Very sketchy. And we were wise to wait.

"A couple minutes of good ol' boy chit chat, and a number of them started lighting these kinds of torches that they had brought with them. Now I was eighty-seven years old at the time, and I've lived in the South my whole life. You see a bunch of White boys out at night lighting torches in an abandoned parking lot, and it doesn't take long to think, well, this could be some kind of Klan thing. Mind you, I've known a number of folks over the course of my life who were Klan, and they were basically good people. Maybe a little more of a hard edge than other acquaintances of mine. But certainly not bad people. It was just their thing. It was never something I went in for; the atmospherics weren't to my liking. But it was something that people did, and I never really held it against them. So while I didn't have a good feeling about this little meeting going on, at the same time I was interested to hear exactly what it was going to be about. And I didn't see any hoods or crosses yet, so we just held back where we were for a spell.

"So they lit up their torches. In the torchlight, I'd say there were around fifty or sixty guys there. One of the crew, who must have been the organizer or leader or what have you, moved to the front and brought the gathering to order. Still staying in the dark, really being careful to stay out of the torchlight, Lucius and I edged in closer towards the gathering so that we could see and hear better what was going on. As we got close enough to see, a couple of things struck me, really surprised me, right away. First, you know how I just said that it was a hardcore kind of crowd? Well, while from a distance it sounded and looked like that, once you got in a little closer, you could see that part of the crowd was like that, but a good part of it didn't look much different from what you look like,

Mordecai, or what I looked like before I turned old. That was a surprise to me. You know, decently dressed people with clean haircuts and no immediately obvious tattoos like you see all these young redneck idiots getting nowadays. Regular people like you'd see at the grocery store or the pharmacy.

"Second thing that surprised me was the gentleman who started talking, the leader. Well, he looked like someone's son or grandson who maybe came up in Buckhead, going to Peachtree Presbyterian or one of the other establishment churches, gone to Westminster or Pace for high school, and maybe gone on to Georgia or Alabama or some other SEC school. Like that. He just looked like a frat boy who'd graduated to some kind of different notion of himself and the world than I believe and hope and pray most of his frat brothers probably did. And he sounded smart, I have to say. Now realize, Mordecai, I'm not a political philosopher. And some of what this young fella was saying, I knew it was out there on the edge. But he wasn't frothing-at-the-mouth, and he used big words, and his sentences were well put together."

"Well, we snuck just a bit closer. And sure enough, I actually recognized, around the outside edges of the crowd, a couple people I thought I knew. Not my generation, but fifty and sixty- year-old men who were known in the community and had come up in good families and had respectable lives. These were fellas who if I told you their names you'd probably know who they were. I'm not going to tell you because it's their own business, but these weren't people who spent their whole life underground or anything like that. In that way, it was kind of like the Klan used to be when I was coming up. Half respectable. Or half of the fellas seemed respectable."

Benno's description of the Klan as half respectable made me cringe, and I noticed it also caught the attention of one of the Black aides who was within earshot, which made me cringe a little more. I figured she'd cut Benno some slack as a resident and an old man; that's the world he came up in. Whether she extended the same slack to me, his audience, I couldn't say.

"So this clean-cut leader boy is talking, and most of the crowd, judging from their faces, was following only a portion of what he was saying. The more establishment looking fellas would occasionally nod their heads. The more redneck part of the crowd just seemed a little antsy, you know, shifting their feet like they'd been standing a little too long. But they were also putting on their best 'I get it' kind of faces even if they didn't. He was talking about the history and dominance and superiority of European culture.

And White culture. This and that and the other and philosophy and all this kind of thing. I'd say his style was kind of like a young assistant professor at a university who maybe just heard he was about to get tenure. A young man full of himself, but not without an idea or two. And you know how sometimes when someone looks like he thinks he's got something important to say, people will listen to him even if they're not sure about it or if they don't really understand what he's saying. I'd say there was some of that going on there.

"But then he said a couple of things, and this little crowd, well, it just went mad-ass crazy. He got into the threats to the White European domination. And he said something like 'Every time one of our women is raped by a Black man, all of White civilization is being raped.' Well, it was like these dudes all at once got stuck with an electric cattle prod. Some of them may not have understood what the hell he was talking about before, but they sure as hell understood now. And they let out the big whoops and 'goddam niggers' and what have you, just like you might expect. Whether they were the hard-looking ones or the country club looking ones, they were all in on it. 'Goddam niggers.'

"He said more stuff like this. He started in on how the niggers -- he quickly took up the term once the crowd had -- how for too long the niggers and the wet-back illegal Spics and Joses and everyone like that, how for too long they'd been taking jobs and opportunities and wealth that the White man rightfully had earned and deserved. He said it had gone on long enough, and it had to stop, all this affirmative action and playing patsy cakes with losers and criminals like we owe them something. When the truth was, as we all knew, and as any rational man knew, that the White man, that we, capital W capital E, were the ones who were owed! The niggers and everyone else owed us for near everything they got, and without the completely stupid, baseless generosity of a sorry-ass White establishment over decades and decades, these neanderthals, these animals wouldn't be much further along than they were in 1865. It had to stop!

"Well, that crowd just got all up in a heat, in a frothy heat. It was like the mention of niggers and neanderthals and 1865 was a call to arms. You couldn't tell whether they were more full of joy or anger. Like literally, Mordecai, they would be smiling and sneering, cheering and really growling at the same time. It just made me wonder -- and I've asked myself this question so many times before

-- but why are these folks so angry? What in the world do they have to be this angry about? I mean we've pretty much ruled the roost here for the last four hundred years. And you might think affirmative action is unfair or wrong. I get it. But good god, look around! I just don't understand all that anger. All that anger, all that fear. I just don't understand it. I don't know, maybe there's something wrong with me, maybe I'm missing something. But I never felt it, and I don't get it. And them, they were just like a pack of monkeys or something. The leader would say 'hoo hoo', and everyone would respond 'heh heh, hee hee'. 'Hoo hoo,' 'heh heh.' Like that, with the same kind of husky, gruff sound to it as you'd expect to hear from a monkey tribe. Just mad-ass crazy. And then he'd throw something in about the Jews, about your people Mordecai, you know, controlling everything and stealing from the pure Whites what's rightfully theirs. And then the monkey tribe would yell back 'hoo, hoo, hoo, hoo, hoo!' Crazy. Like they were in a fever with that anger. Mind you, this was all a few years ago, before we elected our current president. And this was out there then, Mordecai. These folks were out there feeling the way they felt well before they got the message that maybe it was okay to. Good or bad, you could say they were ahead of that curve. 'Nigger, nigger, nigger.' Gets 'em all riled up and ready."

He detected from my face, I guess, that the word made me uncomfortable. I was cognizant again of the Black employees at the Home, and also of the taboo status of those six letters in polite society.

"Mordecai, I know that nigger is not a word that people hear much nowadays, and that people get all skittish and offended when they hear it. And I understand all that. I hope it doesn't bother you my saying it, but that's what these guys were saying. These are the guys that keep that word going. Now me? Other than the meanness behind it, I'll be honest: I never really had an issue with it. Not in political terms. It's just another word like negroes or negras or coloreds. I don't happen to use it and never used it because to me it's an ugly sounding word. Understand me -- I don't like the *feeling* that's usually attached to it either, that's also true, one hundred percent true. Too much anger. Too much hate. We don't need all of it. But beyond that, Mordecai, it's just an ugly word to me. Nigger. Sounds like something you pull out of your nose -- a big, nasty nigger. It's that nig sound. I don't like it. Nig nig nig. Ugly. And with a meanness, yes, also with a meanness."

I'd never heard quite a such a discourse on the aesthetics of the word "nigger." I couldn't say it was a repudiation of the term, but it wasn't an endorsement either. Benno was ninety, and like many who have reached these riper ages, he didn't hold back. His brain would send a message to his tongue, and from his mouth that message would issue forth -- good, bad, or other. "How did Lucius react?" I asked, "to the crowd, the word, the whole thing?"

"Well, the crowd made him a little edgy, a little jittery. But that was par for the course. Lucius, he's never been a big one for the crowds. But as to the name, the word, the anger -- that didn't fluster him much either. I'd say not at all. He was like me you know, old, and he had heard about everything you could hear and was well past the time of life that he'd get too stirred up or hot and bothered. So long as he didn't see anything like a noose hanging from a tree, he was pretty much at peace. And even then, he knew that he was mine, that I owned him, and that I would do whatever I had to do as a gentleman to protect what was mine. And I believe -- I certainly hope -- that gave him some comfort."

Again, that was classic Benno. He'd say things, and you would hear them, and you wouldn't know who you were supposed to be rooting for. You wouldn't know if he and Lucius were on the same side, the same team, or whether that was a morally perverse thought, practically implausible, and shameful to have even thought. But because he loved Lucius, and seemed so comfortable with what he was saying -- and also because it wasn't a hundred percent clear how much if any of this really happened -- you tended to roll along with it.

"Well, unfortunately, I guess we had edged in a little too close to the rally. I didn't think we were inside the torch-lit area, but maybe we were. What happened was that one of the guys at the outside of the group turned around to spit, and when he looked up he saw us. He paused there for a second, and then he said, 'Benno? Is that you? Benno Johnson?' he said. Well, I was caught. I took a step forward so I could see who he was. It was one of my old-time golf partners. I won't tell you his name, but let's call him John Smith for our purposes. He had been one of the younger members of our playing group. We had probably twenty of us who would go out once or twice a week. I would guess John was around fifteen or twenty years younger than me.

"'Good evening, John', I said.

"'Good evening, Benno!' he responded. Well, he was excited to see me. 'Mighty fine to see you here! Welcome to our monthly get together!' He sized me up, 'Benno, what the heck are you wearing, man?'

"'Oh. Yes. That's a bit of a story actually, John' I said. 'Bit of a paddling excursion gone awry, you might say.' Well, he commented on how I might be too old for solo trips down the river at this stage of the game. And I replied that, actually, my boy Lucius had been out there with me. I gestured toward Lucius, and he took a small step forward and nodded his head to John.

"'Well, I'll be! Lucius is still with you! Good to see you, boy!' Lucius nodded again and bowed slightly as I had trained him. All might have been well except for another one of the crowd overheard us talking and turned around and saw Lucius.

"'What's a fuckin' nigger doin' here!' this one yelled. John tried to explain the situation, but once the other fella had uttered the magic word and a few other people in the crowd on the outskirts heard it and also turned around, it was the beginning of a situation that was going to get out of control fast. And that's the direction it headed. Three people, then seven people, then ten people all yelling 'Who's the Nigger!' 'What's that Nigger doin' here!' Before long, the youthful leader caught on to our presence at the back. Well, he was pleased as punch. 'Well, well, well,' he said, 'What have we here this evening, gentlemen? Has fortune favored us with a live Nigger for our entertainment and fulfillment? Cast your torchlight in the darkie's direction, brothers! Let's see what we have!' He then let out a laugh that I could only describe as demonic. I wasn't a hundred percent convinced anything was going to happen to Lucius. But I doubted my ability to turn away what was becoming an angry mob, and so I decided it would be prudent to pull the plug on our involvement in the proceedings forthwith.

"Lucius had already taken a couple of steps back into the darkness. His natural instincts were telling him it was time to flee. The crowd on our edge of things was growing, which is to say everybody was moving over towards where we were, holding their torches. That anger -- it was bigger than me, it was bigger than John. The 'Nigger' chants grew louder and hotter and closer. Mordecai, I could smell the word, I could smell the anger on their breath. I turned around and called out to Lucius who was already another twenty paces further back. I called out with all I had over the noise of the crowd, 'Place One! Place One!' and I held up one finger so he could see even if he couldn't hear. He nodded and held up one finger in response. His eyes were huge and terrified. And he took off into the woods.

"John was trying to mutter some kind of apology to me, but I couldn't make out what he said against the chaos. The sight of Lucius taking off running into the woods actually ignited the crowd to an even more rabid level. Around half of them took off after him with their torches held high. A full mad-ass monkey tribe racing after Lucius. 'Hoo hoo hoo hoo!!!' The anger. The power of that anger."

I could tell it actually stumped him. The anger. He shook his head. "What did you do?" I asked.

"I didn't really know exactly what to do, to be honest. You might be surprised to hear me say it, but I felt Lucius would make it back. Yeah, there was a pack of animals on his tail, but like I said, Lucius was at home in nature. One way or another, I felt like he would make it back. Was I worried? Yeah. *Heck* yeah. It was not a situation we had encountered before. And mind you, this a relationship, him and me, that goes back to the 1930s, for goodness sake! And here we are in 2014 with a Negro President and everything else, and now's the time that we get to deal with this! No, I didn't know exactly what to do, but I decided to make my own slow way into the woods along with the crazies. Maybe I'd be there if they caught him and try to talk sense in some way. Or maybe I would just keep stumbling forward back to our meeting place. That was my hope."

"Yeah. Place One. Is that a...well, what is that? What's that mean?"

"Place One, Mordecai, is a place you know quite well. We always said if something like this happened, we would find each other in Place One. That's what we decided to call it. You would probably call it by a less mysterious name like 'the swamp across the street.'"

"That was your backup plan? To go to the swamp? Why couldn't you have just gone back to your house?"

"Mordecai, with that kind of crowd after Lucius, with that kind of anger in the crowd, well, it just seemed like the safe place to go. Plus, I figured that *they* would figure that my old friend John would know where we went, so I didn't want to go back home for that reason either."

"So, the swamp."

"Yes, the swamp. You might say Lucius had some connections there."

"In the swamp."

"Yes. In the swamp. We actually stayed there for a short spell."

One of the Black aides from the Home had come over and was pointing at her watch. It had actually started to grow dim outside through the windows. Benno had his assigned appointments of the early evening to attend.

"But I guess I'll have to tell you about that next week."

Carefully, gracefully, with just a little help, he got up from the armchair, gave me a restrained but rakish kind of wave and was off.

Chapter 5

After my visits with Benno, I would spend chunks of the following week reflecting on his story, soaking it in fully. And as I remember it and record it here, I feel myself again soaked with it, marinating in it, one serving at a time just like when he first served it to me. Lucius had "connections" in the swamp. Benno knew how to hang the teaser out there. "Connections" in the swamp, whatever that meant.

The rally or conclave that set Benno and Lucius swampward -- sitting here today, three years later, and knowing what's come to pass in our country, it's like having glimpsed the early stirrings of a storm that's now blown up and spun out of control. It tells you that the elements were always there, just like the warm, moist Gulf air and the cool, dry Canadian air are always in circulation even if they don't meet under the precise circumstances and curl into a tornado. Now the tornado blows hard.

A nice, polite, clean cut, handsome young man said hello to me one evening not long ago while I was taking back in the garbage. By his looks and manner and the fact that I'd noticed he was stopping at all the houses on the block, I made him out to be a candidate for office, and I was right. By circumstance, he could have been a salesman of another sort, but by bearing he was a politician. And I don't mean that as a bad thing. I'm one who believes that the great majority, really all but a small minority, of elected officials pursue office and then represent us for good and noble reasons. They want to make the world a better place, and politics, from classical times until today, has been a way to do that. Do I think many are also driven by personal demons to strive after these positions? I do. That's okay by me. We're none of us perfect. Good luck finding many acts undertaken without any blemish of perverse origin or ulterior motive, without any chance of collateral pain.

So this politician called out to me while I was walking away from the street with the garbage can. "Excuse me, sir!" he called out from the street, just loud enough for me to hear but not loud enough to surprise or offend. He introduced himself to me and told me he was running as a Republican for the state legislature. He had a good handshake, good eye contact. He asked for my vote, told me the day of the election, told me it was important. He had done a great job getting his lawn signs up all over the extended neighborhood. This showed strength, organization, diligence. I'm a Democrat, but he impressed me.

He had given me a couple pieces of paper. One was a nice glossy campaign flier that highlighted him, his wife, his dogs (rescue dogs, it was made clear), and his platform: lower taxes, higher growth, less government, more freedom. Hard to argue with that. It's standard issue Republican, but so what; it's the right basic idea, aspiring in the right direction.

However, the other piece of paper he gave me -- that I held against him. It was his personal campaign card. On one side, in red, white, and blue, and underlined with three stars, it repeated his name and the office he was running for, all in caps. On the other side, it gave his contact information, a sentence about his long connection to the district, and then italicized across the bottom in two lines it said this: *"Christian, Husband, Dad of Two Rescue Labs, Graduate of Ole Miss and the University of Georgia Law School, Conservative Republican Fighting for You."*

Christian. That's the first quality that recommended him for office. By the ordering of the list and the conventions of rhetoric, his Christianness was apparently more important than his being a husband, a rescue dog owner, or even well-educated. His ideology and determination, coming last, were arguably on a par with his being Christian on the list of reasons he thought he should get my vote, so I'll give him that.

But "Christian." What does that say? Or, better, what was he saying? That being Christian is the most important quality or qualification to serve in public office and represent fellow citizens of all faiths? Have you ever seen, could you ever imagine a similar campaign card with a similar list of candidate traits that starts with "Jew"? Is someone who is not Christian less fit to serve as a rule?

Moreover, between his name and the photos of him on his material, this particular candidate was about as likely a Christian as you could find. No one would look at his stuff and say, "I wonder if that nice looking young man is a Muslim." Or, "What a nice looking Hindu couple." So not only did he look like a White Christian, not only was his name old-line vanilla, but he was, in fact, Christian, which you already knew, so really what he wanted to tell you was he's *good*, evidently in a way that someone who didn't, or couldn't, lead off with "Christian" wasn't likely to be.

Yes, he and others can get away with this "one of us" type signaling. He might not even have been fully aware of what he was doing. "Christian" is used so regularly as a positive adjective in this part of the country that he might not even have understood how divisive it is, how un-American its implications are, particularly when deployed in the context of public life. But make no mistake -- this "one of us" and "ain't we special" type stuff is a close cousin to the message Benno and Lucius heard in that lot a few years ago. And it's a close cousin to what's flying out of that storm I was just describing. He's complicit in all of that.

But then there's this. When I told my college-aged daughters about Benno and Lucius, they told me I shouldn't tell the story to anyone else because the whole notion of it was too offensive -- an old man and a slave, *today*. And if I not only told it, but let on that I liked Benno, people would think I was racist -- not just complicit in racism, but racist.

That being said, let me say this: when Benno told me about that night with him and Lucius in that parking lot, I couldn't help but note that the one person in the story with no racial animus was the one person in the story who would tell you he owned a slave. I noted it then, and I point it out now because it's interesting, it got me thinking. It made me ask why.

You might be asking if I just endorsed the revival of slavery. What *I'm* asking is why we ask Blacks when they'll get over slavery, but don't ask some Whites when they'll get over the *end* of slavery, when they'll stop whining about that peculiar umbilical cord being cut.

We are none of us pure and all of us complicit -- in something, against someone. But if the choice is being mute, I'll opt for complicit. Because there's always more story to tell.

Part Two - The Swamp

Chapter 6

"Hey, son. Good to see you. Good Shabbos! How about we sit outside today. It looks lovely out."

Thusly did Benno greet me the following Saturday after services. He was right; it was lovely out -- a springtime Saturday morning, the day not yet hot, the air cleared of the first burst of pollen. It was sunny and green and blossomy pink and blue. One of the aides helped Benno up, and we walked past the back of the lobby, down a short hallway and out the door to a nice patio area. It was set up with cushioned all-weather chairs arranged for sun protection either underneath a few trees or around tables with umbrellas. The main campus of the Jewish Community Center was right next door, so residents of the Home and their guests could sit and watch and listen to people, younger and young, playing tennis or soccer or baseball or splashing in the pool. And if they wanted, these young actives could look back at the old and slow and infirm sitting in the shade, just a little downhill from them, on the other side of the fence. We set ourselves down at one of the tables with an umbrella. The aide went back inside.

"So, did you have a good week?" Benno asked me. I answered that I did.

"Business good?"

"Thanks, for asking," I replied. "Yes, it's rolling along."

"Good! That's good."

We had a quiet moment or two. Benno looked off towards the JCC fields, smiled a somewhat absent smile, took a few meaningful sounding breaths, smiled that smile again, then looked back at me and said once more, "Good. That's good."

I could tell he was at least a little out of sorts, which for him was quite noticeable since he typically inhabited each moment so fully and with such ease. "How are *you* doing today, Benno?" I asked.

"Oh, I'm fine. Fine, Mordecai. Thank you, for asking."

He didn't add to the perfunctory response, so after a moment I continued, "I hope you won't mind my saying, but you seem a bit nervous today. What's up?"

He nodded his head slowly, steadily, and said, "Well, I suppose I am at that."

"Why?"

Another pause, then, "Well, I like you. I like you, Mordecai, and I'm afraid you're gonna think I'm crazy."

Of course, there were reasons to think he *was* crazy. His whole story seemed to emerge from an alternate reality. But we'd already come pretty far with it together, so it was alarming and, I must say, at some level titillating, to only now hear him raise the issue of "crazy." My curiosity was piqued, and, bizarrely, all that had come before instantly seemed more credible.

"Crazy?" I asked. "Why?"

"Place One! That's why. Place One! Son, this story is about to turn mighty strange. Hell, you might already think it's strange, but it's about to get a good deal stranger."

"Well, okay. I'm game. I'll hear you out."

"I mean, I know the rest of this is gonna sound crazy. It sounds crazy to *me* when I think back on it. Even just the sound of it in my own head when I'm remembering it sounds crazy. Never mind actually *speaking* it. And it seemed crazy while it was happening. But it happened. It happened, Mordecai. So crazy or not, it's what I lived through. I wouldn't believe it if I hadn't. But I did, so I do."

"All right," I answered. "I understand. Place One. Tell me about it."

Benno gathered himself up, took a deep breath, let it out, and began.

"Place One, Mordecai. Place One. First of all, let me tell you that I made it back there that night, on foot. It might've taken an hour, might've taken three hours. I can't say; time became blurry for me that night. But I made it back. More bedraggled. More pathetic, you could say, old and spent as I was. But I actually felt pretty good. Pretty good, I'd have to say. I made it back, after all.

"And Lucius was there as well. Already there. He made it back like I knew he would. Oh, he had some stories he told me about how close they got -- and they got pretty damn close! But he kept moving, deployed some tactics to discourage and dissuade and *evade* his pursuers, and made it back. We were both tired, exhausted. But we were both energized, too. Adrenaline, I guess. Didn't know I had any left. But it'd been pumping, and it still was some.

"I went down the slope, you know, on the edge of the street, and down into the swamp. And Lucius was right there. You know how it is -- it's a forest floor down there, around fifteen feet below street level, and then there's a perimeter of that forest that's around twenty yards deep until you get to the swampy, pond area around the size of a football field. So we reconnoitered there on the forest floor.

"It was dark, and you've got a lot of treefall down there. Without Lucius, I'd have just spent the night tripping and falling. But Lucius has got great night vision. Really *remarkable* night vision. And I should probably tell you something about that. And Mordecai, here's where it might start sounding odd to you. But all I can do is tell it."

"Shoot."

"I will. So it's like this, and this is just how Lucius described it to me. And knowing him just about my whole life and seeing his set of skills tends to support his account, as...unorthodox as it is. And certainly our next couple days together, in the swamp and thereabouts, bears him out fully. He has a different understanding of evolution. It's not the one they teach in school. Of course he never went to school, and I don't know where he picked his ideas up. I've assumed they were passed down as a kind of folk tradition if you will. Parent down to child. And I don't know if this understanding was particular to his family, or if all coloreds know about it. In any event, it's like this: you have two tracks. One track is similar to the evolution ideas you'd be familiar with. You know, coming up out of the primordial soup; simple organisms; more complex organisms; and on up to humans. But the interesting thing about Lucius's version -- well, there are a couple interesting things -- but the first one is that the chain of evolution caps out at the Black man. That's the top of the chain, or I guess you could say the end of that track. The White man -- you and me, Mordecai -- it's not really clearly drawn out *how* we got here. Maybe the end of a different, parallel track. Maybe just kind of dropped here. It's not clear. But we're different, from a different process. And that differentness, that's part of why they respect us, even fear us some. You hangin' in there so far?"

"I am. It *is* different. I might have guessed it was guns that made them respect us, but I'm following you."

"*Yes!* But there you have it. And here's the other interesting part, and this is the part that was proved out for me the next two days. How can I explain this -- well, let me say it like this: Lucius,

124

my boy Lucius, he himself in some pertinent measure lived through each of those stages of evolution. From small amoeba-like critter to bigger critter to tadpole, frog, fish, and whatever else all the way on up to Negro human. You know, sprung legs somewhere along the way, went upright -- the whole thing. And not only that -- and, really, *because* of that -- the Negro is connected in like a soul way to all those critters and all those animals he's passed on through. *And*, he retained the ability to communicate with them, *all* of them seems like. So that's what I'm meaning when I say he had connections in the swamp. He *knew* them. Not like I know you, but like we know other people we see. You understand? Like we know we share the same basic wiring and we can communicate somehow. That's how it was. He shared wiring with all these creatures at some level and could communicate with them. Talk to them, really. And they'd understand and he'd understand, too.

"And this is the common understanding of Blacks?" I doubtfully asked.

"No! Or, I don't think so. I don't know, really. Like I said, it could be a particular folk wisdom to Lucius's people. I really don't know. But I tell you what -- we got down in that swamp, and he was talking and interpreting with those animals. With all of them.

"And *you* could understand what they said, too?"

"That's an excellent question, son. *Excellent* question. This is how it was: first thing to say is that I could understand that they understood. It was obvious by the way the back and forth between Lucius and all of them transpired. Occasionally, Lucius would tell me what they were talking about as they were talking. But the other thing, and you'd really have to call this magic, is that when Lucius would take my hand, hold my hand, I could *understand* what they were saying! Now it was peculiar, because I couldn't actually understand or translate the actual *words*. What I mean to say is the *sounds* that they were making were not *words* to me that I understood. But I understood what they were saying. And it wasn't even that I just got the gist of it, you know; I really understood what they were saying. *But*, even then, even when Lucius was holding my hand, I couldn't communicate back to them. I would offer a thought to Lucius about whatever the situation might have been, and I had a sense that they *might* have understood what I was saying. But really, if I started talking to them, they would just look at Lucius. It was almost like 'Who's the crazy 'ol White man, and why's he making those talking sounds?'" Which was a question that I, Tree Weissman, was at that very moment tempted to ask myself. In

Benno's defense, though, he *had* warned me it would start sounding crazy, or crazier; if nothing else, he was delivering on the warning.

"So that night when we arrived, it was a nice, warm summer night. You need to understand that the toads were by far the most numerous critters there. If it was a democracy down in the swamp, which in some ways I suppose it was, the toads would run the show. Little though they are, and vulnerable on account of their littleness, they for sure had the numbers. So the first group of toads that sees us, there's a big ruckus amongst them. They're making their various sounds, and Lucius is responding to them. Lucius actually spoke in the sound of the toads and the frogs. He had picked up that language facility along the way. One of the toads starts to assert himself as the leader, and that's the one Lucius describes our situation to. His name was Jimmy."

"Jimmy?"

"Yeah. Later on that night as we were laying down to sleep, I asked Lucius what the deal was with the leader frog. And real calm and patient, Lucius says to me 'You mean, Jimmy? Well, first of all, dats no frog; dats a toad. And second of all, Jimmy just plain got his self to be da leader. He's one da older ones of da toads, and they come to respect him over da long time.'

"And as I got to know Jimmy over the next few days, I could see why: he was a toad with spunk, real spunk. He spoke his mind clearly and with attitude. I'd almost say he struck me like a ghetto toad. He had that kind of *swagger* to him, small and toad-like as he was, but still. I'm telling you, he had a sense of command to him.

"But what was interesting the way it played out was, that once we got there and once Lucius struck up an initial rapport with Jimmy, out of the water and up to the forest floor leapt this big 'ol bullfrog. His name was Marty. It was like he just fell out of the sky, he jumped in from so far away. What I didn't describe to you properly, Mordecai, is the size differential in these critters. Tell me if you already know this, but toads around here tend to be much smaller than frogs. A toad might grow to be a couple inches long. Same goes for most tree frogs. Frogs, on the other hand, *true* frogs like a bullfrog, like Marty, could be six inches long easy. And the toads, they mostly make smaller sounds like what you would think a cricket or other insect might make. Truth is, until I spent this time with them, I thought most of the sounds coming out of the swamp at night were crickets. In fact, turns out it's toads, and tree frogs. Bullfrogs, on the other hand, make more of the big croak sound that you might typically think of. Even a little moo in it. There's another frog that sounds like a crazy old man laughing. Like something out of a fun house. So Marty comes flying out of the sky, essentially leaping over the whole assembled crowd, and lands, I kid you not, smack dab on top of three little toads who let out these scared little chirps and kind of shuffle left and right.

"So then 'Croak,' says Marty. A big 'ol moo sounding croak. And the whole toad cacophony quiets down just like that. And when the toads quiet down, it's like the whole swamp pretty much goes quiet. You can hear an *actual* cricket. And so what happens is that Jimmy and Marty sort of square off with each other. Marty, he wants to know what's going on and who we are. So Lucius says a word or two, but Jimmy asserts himself then. He explains to Marty that we need to be staying there for a spell. And that the toads have agreed to host us. Then Marty says, 'Well, that's great that it's okay with you toads, but you've got to run it by me, Jimmy, my boy.' Well, it went from quiet to quieter then, and there was a moment of doubt or fear or some kind of amphibian anxiety that swept over the toads. But then Jimmy, cool as a cucumber, let out a little chuckle, whereupon all the other toads broke into the same kind of chuckle, so that it was a regular laugh track there for a second. And Jimmy says, 'Marty, my slick friend, I was about to hop over to the pond to tell you what was happening before you leapt on in here, nearly crushing three of my little brothers in the process, mind you. All the grace of a possum. But never mind that. This is the plan how I see it: they stay here with us on the leafy floor, and we only head on over to you and the real wet stuff if we need to burrow down and hide for any reason. What do you say, what do you say, what do you saaaaaay, my slimy, magnificent brother?' He was well spoken, that Jimmy. Maybe over-repeated himself for emphasis, but well spoken. Still, Marty sat there for a minute. He let out a couple moderate toned croaks, flashed his tongue a few times, and croaked again. Jimmy added, 'And, *and* Marty, I don't reckon we'll have quite as hard a time from the crows and hawks and such while these two strapping creatures are in residence. Or the snakes. Am I right or am I right?' So Marty took that in. If you ask me, he was sold on the proposition, but he drew the moment out for dramatic effect. And sure enough, he said okay. He said it without enthusiasm, mind you, but 'okay.' He let out another one of his moo-croaks, and bounded back towards the water. Didn't welcome us or anything at all. It wasn't consistent with his bullfrog image. But once he left, Jimmy started laughing and all the other toads started laughing. They considered it another manifestation of their superiority over

Marty and his crew. And so we ended our arrival with everyone in high spirits.

We bedded down for the night, just like Jimmy described, in the soft leaves on the forest floor. They were a bit moist and carried a smell that was very earthy, that you might describe as, well, forest floor. Mordecai, my bronchial passageways have their good days and their other days, and I was a little concerned that the whiff of forest carried with it a whiff of mold which might cause me some problems getting to sleep. Also, I was a bit concerned of the insect population regarding us as the grandest, slowest, dumbest food of the season. But turned out that all was well, and I was fine. The frogs and their lightning tongues being all around us was a convincing deterrent to the insects. And somehow or another, the moisture on the leaves just didn't bother me. I felt remarkably in my element after a couple minutes there next to Lucius in amongst the amphibians, our new friends. You know amphibian literally means having two lives. I looked it up when I got back home. Having two lives, or both lives. So you might actually say I was an amphibian, Mordecai! Me and Lucius fit the bill! We were our own kind of amphibians. In the swamp with Lucius and the critters, and as humans as well. And especially when Lucius held my hand and I could understand what all the little critters around us were saying, I felt like I belonged.

"It was a beautiful night. And though we were lying on our backs on the ground with trees obscuring the sky, it felt like the brightest, most lively night once we'd settled in there. There was an almost full moon that night; it shined down and reflected off of the pond just to our side, and we were covered in that soft reflection. And as my eyes became accustomed to the dark, and as I came to understand where the toads and frogs were stationed on the ground and up in the trees, what at first had been dark and camouflaged started to come to life, moment by moment. The frogs and toads are nocturnal, of course, and the more I looked and the more I saw them, the more I could see how their eyes really almost shined. Well, not almost -- they really did shine. And so as I lay there with Lucius, looking up at the sky, looking up at the sky through those trees, it was as though there were a thousand tiny lanterns lighting up the air around us. It was all deep navy blue and white and yellow. Laying there looking up, it was almost like we were sleeping inside a snow globe of a forest and a pond at night. And when you shook it, it would light up and come to life.

"And then a swamp symphony began. To my fully human ears, it was just the sound of a thousand frog chirps and squeaks and burps and whistles. And of course I couldn't make heads or tails of what they were actually saying. They could have been declaring war on each other for all I knew. 'Holy cow,' I said to Lucius. 'What's this big noise about?'

"'Oh, dats right!' he answered cheerfully. 'I done forgot you doesn't speak frog. Give me yo hand.' He chuckled as he took my hand. 'There, now. Take a listen. Jimmy and his crew singin' now.'

"I listened like he said, and unmistakably, and how it could be unmistakable to me is one of those inexplicable things, but unmistakably, Jimmy's crew of the many and the small had started up singing. It was past mating season, so they weren't singing their love songs to one another. No, it was a different kind of song. I don't know, you might call it political, or a camp song maybe. It was definitely a song of the *group*. They sung it to make a point and enjoyed themselves while they were making it. Though my ears had become attuned to their language, I couldn't really tell you what the melody was. I could detect undulation in their tone with certain lyrical developments, but if you asked me to hum the melody to you, that I couldn't do. But the words I recall. They went like this:

In the swamp we are so small. Just teeny, helpless things.

But we have you in our thrall, our tongues upon your wings.

There are frogs, real fat and tall, who croak like cows might sing.

But we think you look real small, your brains are teeny things!

"Well, they sang it over and over again, which is how I could remember it, and each time reaching a crescendo. If I was understanding it correctly, it was a sweet little piece of pointed rhetoric, with one jab against the insects and another against the bullfrogs. And really, over and over they sang it, like a camp song, or a battle chant.

"They had the stage to themselves, so to speak, for a few minutes. But then, here comes that moo-croak of the bullfrogs. Lower, more resonant in tone, compared to their smaller cousins. And much simpler in message:

We are the bullfrogs

We are the bullfrogs

We are the bullfrogs --

And you're NOT!

"Over and over, Marty's crew belch-mooed out this simple but I must say quite effective song in response. And at the end of each 'NOT', they would all break out into a big garble garble of bullfrog laughter. Jimmy and his people kept right on singing, mind you. So it had the effect of a most unusual and discordant round, one on top of the other, and one trying to top the other.

"And then, most peculiar, Mordecai, those laughing frogs I described to you, the ones that sound like a crazy man laughing by himself at a bus stop or something like that, they start in with their own song in that mad hyena kind of heh heh tone of theirs:

Jimmy sings and Marty, too. Heh heh heh heh heh.

What is singing going to do. Heh heh heh heh heh.

When a car's on top of you. Heh heh heh heh heh.

Or you're stuck to someone's shoe. Heh heh heh heh heh.

"This was not a mood lifter, this song. But it did have the effect of bringing the Jimmy and Marty crews together in a loud, raucous chorus of boos. I had the sense that it wasn't something they hadn't heard the crazy frogs singing about before. Everyone was more or less singing their own refrain. And one over the other over the other. They all seemed to be enjoying themselves. *I* was enjoying myself. I looked over at Lucius, and he was smiling as well. I could see his eyelids growing heavy, and I realized I was growing sleepy, too. I closed my eyes, adjusted my hand in Lucius's, and drifted right off to sleep. And I dreamed that Lucius and I had joined the singing, had entered the Fellowship of the Frog Chorus -- that's what it was called in my dream. We were singing 'Swanee River.' In my dream, they all stopped totally silent to hear us singing, and then picked up again as before, with us and our song joined right in.

"I woke up, or was woken up, at first light, barely first light. There was an outbreak of frog talk of some sort all around me. It was disorienting for a minute, but then I remembered where I was, and I reached to find Lucius's hand so that I could understand what was going on. Lucius had woken up as well, and he took my hand as we both sat up. 'What are they saying?', I asked him. But before he could even answer, I figured it out. 'Possum Possum Possum' is what they were saying.

"'There's a possum comin','" Lucius said.

"So I said, 'I hear them, Lucius. I hear them. That's trouble, I guess?'

"And he says, 'Yessuh. Big trouble. Dem possums sump'n mean!'

"So I said, 'Well, they *look* mean, that's for sure. And *ugly*. I didn't know they ate frogs, but I guess that's what the kerfuffle is all about?'

"'Yessuh', he says, 'Yessuh, dey do. Dats de kerfufflin'.

"So I told him I didn't know that, and he says to me, 'Like Jimmy was sayin' last night, dey got lotsa da others want to eat da frogs. Da frogs -- dems good food. Like dey say on da TV. Tastes just like chicken.' And he chuckled at that. Turns out anything with a mouth big enough to fit a frog inside likes eating a frog.

"Meantime, Jimmy hopped over. 'People,' he said, 'People, um, so...*do* something!' His tone was hushed but urgent.

"'Like what?' Lucius asked.

"Impatient, Jimmy responded, 'Just be YOU, for cripes sake! Stand up, be seen, *mark* something!'

"'Sho' enough, Jimmy. Sho' enough,' Lucius tells him, and then stands up and says to me, 'C'mon. Let's mark dis here territory. I's needin' to wee wee anyway.'

"Wee wee. That's what he calls it. Funny term for an old timer. So we get up, and we start trying to let go with our streams there, and, well, you know, *both* of us being old, sometimes it takes a second or sixty for the river to flow if you know what I mean. So we're there with our peckers out, and here comes the possum into sight. They are *ugly* critters. Just about the ugliest. And there we are with our peckers out, trying to mark our territory, and here's the possum. And I say to Lucius, 'I'm not feeling the best about hanging out here all exposed right now.' And he says, 'I know what you mean, but here we is.' Meantime, the frogs are all scattering, taking to the trees if they can, and Mister Possum comes up around fifteen feet from us and stops short. He looks us up and down, not scared, more surprised and confused. We're still standing there trying to let loose, the two of us, and Mr. Possum makes a sound, a few sounds, like he's talking to us. At the first moment there, I couldn't understand what he was saying on account of both my hands were occupied. But Lucius started talking back to him, so I gave up on the marking effort and grabbed Lucius's hand.

"'Dats right, Possum. You seein' what you seein', Lucius said.

"And in a real, wretchy kind of nasal voice, Possum says, 'It's been a long night. I wasn't sure. Sorry to bother you. I don't usually see your kind down here. You think you'll stay long?' And then, in a belated effort at manners, he says, 'I mean, welcome, of course. Why are you here? Um, I mean, sorry -- what brings you men here?'

"So right then, Lucius lets his ol' wee wee go, and points it right at the possum. Possum's not close enough so that the urine hits him, but it's arcing out straight at him, and he sort of shuffles back six inches or a foot. And son of a gun, all of a sudden I feel the urge come back and get some relief as well, mark some territory of my own! Lucius says, 'We here cuz we likes to be here, and we likes our frog and toad friends, and we fixin' to stay til we fixin' to leave.' He finished marking his territory, as did I, but we stood there, still holding hands, and each with our johnsons hanging out. Quite a picture we must've been. And with us like that, Lucius continued, 'And I guess *you* fixin' to leave, oh, right about NOW. Is I right?'

"And so Mr. Possum did his kind of shuffle again and said in his nasaly, scratchy voice 'Yes, sir. It's gotten too light for me to be

out. I'll just move along. Thank you, and, um, well, good morning.'
And he skulked his ugly self away.

"So Lucius and I tucked ourselves back into our pants, and
Lord Almighty, did a great frog love ruckus break out. I reached for
Lucius's hand again. They were all chanting 'Lucius, Lucius,
Lucius.' And good fellow that he was, and of generous spirit, Lucius
points to me and says 'Benno.' And they start up with 'Lucius and
Benno! Lucius and Benno!' On and on they go, the frogs and toads,
young and old, all of them. Mordecai, I felt like a hero! A hero of
the swampland, that was me. Never would have thought I had it in
me, Mordecai. Never. And I don't mean to gloat about it. I mean,
Lucius was the key man there. But my fellow amphibians, they
didn't seem to distinguish too much. Soon enough we each around
ten of them that hopped or jumped on top of us, on our legs and
arms and shoulders. Lucius had one land right on top of his *head*."

"Didn't bother you?" I asked.

"No," Benno said. "Not at all. In fact, Lucius and I just
broke up laughing. We laughed and laughed. He reached on top of
his head and cupped that little toad that had landed there into his
hand, and we both looked at it and laughed, laughed, laughed. And
that toad, all the toads and frogs started laughing with us."

"Sounds lovely," I said.

"It *was* lovely. It *was*. And it was still early morning. Just light. And the sun was really just starting to shine in slantwise from the east, from the river side, over and between our houses. It was a blue-sky day, I could see that, up through the jigsaw of branches. Soon enough it would be warming up. But it was a good start to the day."

And as it turned out, it was the end of our day, Benno's and mine. His aide appeared, and his schedule beckoned.

"Hey! See you next week," he said as he headed off.

"See you next week, Benno."

Chapter 7

When I was a kid, I was good at basketball. Tall like a tree, I dominated the overwhelmingly Jewish competition at the New Haven JCC. I was a chunker at that age. An old team picture that one of my teammates recently unearthed shows the team, half on one knee, half standing, all wearing our team t-shirts. Except me. There wasn't a t-shirt large enough for my height and heft. So I'm standing next to the coach, in a completely different short-sleeve shirt, looking badly misplaced, more like his assistant than one of his players. I was probably nine years old then, maybe ten. I would grab rebounds, hold the ball over my head, and observe as little Jewish boys would launch at me, only to bounce off my ample belly and chest and fall to the floor. I could miss four of five consecutive two-foot bank shots, and it didn't matter; no one was going to challenge me for the rebound. I was the Shaq of the realm.

As I got older, I practiced indefatigably, and my skills improved. I was a good, young player. I grew up in an upper-middle class neighborhood. The neighborhood was mostly but not entirely White -- the old FDR ethnic stew of Jews, Irish, Italians, and other Whites of European descent. But there were a few Black families as well, and the neighborhood was all of five blocks away from a large, poor urban neighborhood. Our neighborhood literally sat on top of a hill; the poor neighborhood sat at the bottom of the hill centered on Hillhouse High School, and a mile or so beyond the high school was downtown New Haven and Yale. Hillhouse at one time had been one of the best high schools in the country, a stepping stone to Yale for bright and industrious ethnic Whites. But by the time I was coming up, almost no White families would send their kids there if they had any choice at all. The school was almost entirely Black and Latino. Why it flipped like this I leave to the sociologists, the demographers, the political scientists. It's not a unique story.

And really, it's all just by way of explaining that the basketball played in the driveways of our hilltop neighborhood was of a respectably high caliber. Usually me and my also White next-door neighbor -- he of the adept dribbling and quick release jump shot -- would be shooting around or playing one-on-one in someone else's driveway (for whatever reason, neither of us had a great set-up in our own driveways) and a couple of Black kids would materialize on foot or bike and ask to play. This was pretty much any afternoon or early evening from when we were around eleven to when we were probably fifteen. To ease right into the stereotype, I would say that we were the more skilled shooters, more technique-oriented defenders and rebounders, and they were faster, jumped higher, and were slightly -- only slightly -- more aggressive. These kids were amongst our friends. Whether they lived in the neighborhood or down the hill, I couldn't say. One of them was a really big kid who seemed to show up on a different bicycle almost every day. We couldn't make sense of this until we could. This guy went on to hit six foot eight, two hundred fifty pounds, had a good high school career at one of the very good New Haven programs, and then did some time in jail. I lost track of him long ago, but we were basketball friends. I had blonde hair and a good jump shot, and the Black guys called me Larry Bird.

Why am I telling you this? I'm not sure. But there was something about what Benno said about being an amphibian that's been bouncing around inside my head since he said it, and for whatever reason it brought this story to mind. "Two lives," "both lives" -- there's something in there I can't quite unpack. So I beat around the bush knowing that the bush is there but I just can't see it yet.

Who's Black, and who's White. In 2017, how many drops of Thomas Jefferson's blood, how many strands of his Jeffersonian DNA would make someone his son and not his slave? Would make someone White and not Black. Our first Black president was half White. Who decided he was Black? Well, ultimately he did, perhaps because the culture already had. But why not White? Why not "Other." Why does it matter, and what does it mean, and who decides? Look around. Look at famous people and people you see on the street every day. What "passes" as White today, and what "passes" as Black? All you need to do is open your eyes to see how the old categories have become genetically and cosmetically meaningless. Color-blind love and lust prevail, offspring issue forth, and yet we all cling like madmen to the old binaries, like Gollum grasping after the ring. Not even Black and White are black and white anymore, but we seem not to want to know it.

Here's a little story I made up during a power outage not long ago, by candlelight, waiting with my daughters for the lights to come back on.

Once upon a time, there was a bird and a dog. Not a bird dog, although the dog was of one of the breeds suitable for hunting birds. This particular bird dog, a Flat-Coated Retriever with soft black hair, was no good at hunting. When his first owners tried him out as a retriever on the hunt, he never quite got around to the retrieving part of the job, which was pretty much the entirety of it. He wasn't great at focusing on a task. So his first owners left him at the pound. They didn't want him anymore because he was of no use to them. His new owners couldn't believe they were so lucky to find such a great dog, so beautiful and sweet. They took him home.

The bird was a pigeon. She was grey, blue, and white. I'm not saying those were her only or exact colors, but if you looked at her and had to tell someone what she looked like, those are the colors you would come up with first. She was reasonably healthy looking, not obese as some pigeons get. One of her wings was slightly damaged, so her hunting and scavenging skills were sub-par. Make no mistake, she could fly, but not quite as well as the others. Still, there was enough lower grade, bird-food eligible junk

146

strewn here and there in the neighborhood, that she could do okay -- worms, but not the biggest worms, for example. She didn't have a lot of friends amongst the other pigeons. Sometimes you might notice how pigeons in large groups isolate one of their mates who looks different or has something wrong with him. Well, that's what had happened with this pigeon in this neighborhood. As a result, she was kind of an involuntary loner.

This is how Pigeon and Dog met. Pigeon was foraging for food in Dog's backyard. Dog saw her, and still wired with his breed's ancient instincts, started a happy charge towards Pigeon. Pigeon saw Dog charging at her and attempted her evasive maneuver, but due to her wing damage, she didn't get quite as far away as pigeon guidelines would recommend. She somewhat clumsily landed only a few yards away. In the meantime, Dog had pulled up short of Pigeon's original location. Dog wasn't even really sure why he was charging at Pigeon. Either he had already forgotten, or he never knew. When Pigeon fell to earth a few yards away, Dog looked at Pigeon and Pigeon looked back at Dog and they just stood there like that for a few seconds. Dog commenced with his ritual of excited sniffing but made no further aggressive gestures. Pigeon soaked this in, determined a lack of danger, and said hello. Dog also said hello. So now they had met.

They would repeat this scene in the backyard many times each day. For a while, it was somewhat fraught with fright for Pigeon as she wasn't sure that Dog would remain friendly, counter to what Pigeon knew to be the natural instincts of Dog's type. But day after day, Pigeon became more comfortable. They became good friends and companions in the manner of which they were capable, sharing the yard and shooting the breeze. They exchanged daily pleasantries, commented on each other's habits and odors, and predicted the weather.

Pigeon had asked Dog once or twice to join her on a walk, a little expedition around the neighborhood. There were some places she thought Dog would like. They actually started off once, intent on taking such a trip, before they realized Dog could not leave the backyard. It was fenced. So for a while, the expedition remained a dream deferred.

One day the gate was left open. Dog didn't realize this until some time after he had actually gone ahead and wandered outside the gate. He was consumed with his usual sniffings and other doggish obsessions. It was only when Pigeon saw where Dog had wandered that she realized they finally had their opportunity to go for that walk. She flew over, landed, and said, "Hey, we can go for that walk now." Dog looked up, looked around, and said, "Oh, fun. Let's go." So off they went.

They quickly realized they had a problem. Dog started trotting ahead and soon realized that Pigeon was nowhere in sight. He turned around and called back, "Hey, Pigeon! Why aren't you walking with me?" Pigeon took flight and flew up to where Dog was waiting. "Well, Dog, I just can't walk that fast on these pigeon legs." She sounded a little perturbed. Dog cleverly replied, "Well why don't you fly then? You're faster when you fly, right?" "Good idea," said Pigeon.

So off they went again, Dog happily galloping along and Pigeon taking wing. But soon they realized that they still had a problem. For maybe fifty yards, Dog was able to keep up, but beyond that, he couldn't. Pigeon looked down and realized Dog was nowhere in sight and circled back to where Dog had stopped, his tongue out, panting and tired.

"This is really frustrating," she said. "No matter how slow I fly, I am still way faster than the fastest you can run. I'll need to keep coming back to you and we won't get anywhere!" Dog replied,

"Yeah. And no matter how slow I walk, I'm still way faster than the fastest you can walk. I would have to walk around in circles over and over and over again, and by that time I would get bored and forget what I was even doing! This stinks." Pigeon agreed, so they just stood there for a few minutes contemplating how badly the situation stunk. They had waited so long to go on an expedition together and now it turned out it was impossible. They started heading back to the yard. All at once Dog had an idea. "What if you stand on my back? You're really small and light, and I know it would be easy for me to carry you, and that way we could go for a walk and stay together!" Pigeon said "That's a good idea, Dog! That's the best idea you ever had!" Dog had already sensed he was being smart, but with this affirmation from his friend Pigeon, he felt prouder and happier than he ever had. So Pigeon hopped up on Dog's back, and they went for an absent-minded expedition here and there and who knows where. They got some strange looks from other dogs and birds, and passing cars as well. It wasn't every day you saw a pigeon riding on the back of a dog, after all. Not in these parts, at least. But they had a grand old time of it, gawkers be damned, and returned home just ahead of Dog's family. "That worked really well!" Pigeon said to Dog. "I hope we get a chance to do that again." Dog wagged his tail with glee and replied, "Yeah. Me, too." And then Dog went inside because his family was calling him.

I couldn't tell you exactly why, but this story makes me think of Benno. Him and Lucius and this world and that world. Is there a "this" and a "that" to anything anymore? I don't know. Everything seems real and unreal, chaotic and accidental. This little story was accidental: I was with my girls, we were telling stories, and this one just came out. And yet I think it makes sense -- in its own world, and somehow in ours. I'll be the dog; you can be the pigeon. Or *I'll* even be the pigeon; you can be the dog.

Chapter 8

"Mordecai! Hey! So where were we?" was Benno's greeting as I joined him after services.

"Morning, Benno. Let's see. I think the frog kingdom was just singing your praises."

"Right. Right. After the possum deal."

"That's right."

"Okay. Let's see. Hey! Do you want to go sit outside on the patio again today?" he asked. It was a little warmer this week, and more humid, but Benno was the storyteller, and I was happy to defer.

"Sounds great," I answered. I helped him up, he motioned to one of the aides that we were headed outside, and we made our way to the nice chairs and umbrella where we had sat the week before.

"So it was full morning by then. Lucius and I were feeling good about our first twelve hours or so in the swamp, and Lucius asked me if I wanted to take a walk around. 'Sure,' I told him.

'Sure, that sounds just fine. Like the old days. Take us a little reconnaissance mission, eh?'

"'Dats right, suh,' he said. 'Just like dem old days. Lay of da land and all. See what we see.'

"So off we went. We set off on a northward, upstream heading, to that side of the swamp. Mordecai, have you ever been down there?" he asked me.

"In the swamp?"

"That's right. And also the environs. You ever explore around there at all?"

I told him I hadn't. I'd been down the bank once just to check out what the pond actually looked like up close, but I hadn't ever ventured farther afield.

"Well," he said, "once you get past the pond and the swampy perimeter, if you head north, there's probably a mile of forest before you come up on any houses. Nothing 'til the Deer Run Manor neighborhood. You can just walk along in the forest with the river to your right as you're headed north. It's probably a swath of a quarter mile wide between the river and the road. And a mile straight ahead. And no houses because it's all flood plain."

On our long weekend walks, my dog and I travel the sidewalk on the road side of that area Benno was describing. I would always keep one eye towards the woods because it looked like the kind of area where you might see deer herds, foxes, even a black bear if bears lived around here. In actual fact, I don't think I ever saw anything larger than a squirrel in there. But it was the kind of tract that you still figured could host some impressive wildlife. In the morning, the sun would shine into the forest from the east, the river side, just as Benno had described the sun starting to shine into the swamp. It was nice to look at: all the trees, sunshine, the long shadows, and in a few spots a glimmer of the river all the way on the other side. I nodded in a way that let Benno know I was following him.

"So we're walking along, not far north of the swamp, and Lucius starts up singing. He sings the 'Battle Hymn,' Mordecai, 'The Battle Hymn of the Republic.' Well, I didn't remember us ever singing that one before, not when we were kids and not after. But walking through those woods, you did get the feeling it was the kind of terrain they fought through in the War. You could imagine it there. Other thing that struck me though -- 'Battle Hymn' was the *Union* song. Oh, I guess it's just a well-known hymn by now, but still, it struck me that Lucius knew it because I didn't know *how* he knew it. Anyways, it's a great song, that's for sure. I joined right in, and we just kept on keepin' on like Union soldiers marching through the woods. Good singing. We were probably out there on the move for about an hour.

"When we got back, Jimmy came right over to greet us. There was a sense of urgency about him, Mordecai. I could tell he had an agenda. Jimmy was a frog with an agenda.

"'Where you been, where you been, where you *beeeeen!*' he chirp-croaked at us. So Lucius tells him how we just went out on an expedition, a reconnaissance, out and around the acres on the other side of the swamp.

"'Ohhhh,' Jimmy said, and his Greek frog chorus all squatted there around him chimed in with their own 'ohhhh' as well. And then 'Gooooood,' said Jimmy, and 'goooood' the chorus said. Funny that I remember this detail, but not all the frogs did their 'ohs' and 'goods' in the same key. Some were higher, some were lower. It was like the Oompa Loompa chorus from the Wonka movie. High low, high low, high low. Like that.

"So Jimmy went on, and he told us they had a problem. He told us like it was a *new* problem. Now Mordecai, you know that

155

they didn't just come up with some new problem the morning after me and Lucius showed up, right? What they came up with was a new *solution* -- namely us. Like I say, Jimmy was clever. He knew how to frame the issue.

"So I'm holding Lucius's hand so I can follow, and here's what Jimmy said. He goes 'Guys, guys, *guyyyys*. Guys, we got a problem, a *biggggg* problem here. Maybe you could help!' His voice kind of went up a little as he said 'help,' and he paused and sorta cocked his head a little to one side and looked at us. 'You see, we got a problem here. You know how it's summertime -- you've noticed that, right? Well, this is the time of year (and here he slowed down a bit like maybe we were on the daft side) this is the time of year when our youngsters, you know, I don't know what you call them exactly, but the young ones, well, they're a few months old now, and this is the time of year when they leave the swamp and head out to wherever they're going to head out to and settle into their new lives. You follow? (We nodded our heads, and Lucius made the 'yes' sound). All right, good. So, you know, they've been growing up, learning about life around here, and just generally getting ready to strike out on their own. Well, now they're ready, and they might not come back home for a couple years! Building their own lives. Little frog pioneers. It's part of our greatness as a species.' You could see the little frog chorus behind him getting emotional, their eyes misting up a little. They started blinking a lot, and their frog gullets started to swell out prodigiously. Swell and retract, swell and retract.

"Now, all this time, Mordecai -- and actually it had started happening even earlier, before we set out on our little expedition -- all this time, birds, mostly crows, would fly into the swamp area, pluck up a little frog or toad, carry it away a few yards, and, well, eat it. Right there, Mordecai! Like nothing. Like a normal day. Meantime, everyone else would just kind of carry on with their business like nothing was happening. Then, BOOM! Out of the sky, here comes another one. Sometimes a young heron would actually dive right into the pond and pluck one and then fly off, but usually it was these crows. When I saw it happen a few times earlier in the morning, well, it was jarring. I didn't know what to make of it. But everyone was so happy with our backing down the ol' possum, that I didn't really give it a thought. Because *they* didn't seem to give it a thought. Just chirping and croaking away with us, and BOOM! Here swoops another crow, and with a couple sharp downward pecks, he's got a little froggy in his mouth, and he just basically stands there and eats it. If a bigger frog makes a move towards him, he just grabs his food and flutters on away a few yards and keeps on eating. Some of the frogs and toads emit a kind of mild poison or bad taste, but the crows seem to work their way around it. Doesn't bother 'em. Least not enough to stop. And why would they? They've got easy pickins there! The frogs and toads, their basic game plan is to stay real still and wait for an insect to come by, and then they go ZAP with their sticky tongues, pull it back in, and eat it. They've got no shortage of insects to feed on, but they're literally just sitting there, Mordecai! They have some camouflage helping them out, sure. But their own hunting strategy makes them easy hunting!

"So this is the problem Jimmy's getting around to telling us about. The young frogs are getting ready to set out. Heading wherever. To the Arnaud meadow, or towards the river, or north of the swamp into the woods there where Lucius and I had just been. Somewhere. But meantime, the birds know they're fixing to move, and they're all kind of concentrated there still, still easy pickins, so the birds are loading up. And Jimmy's telling us all this, and the crows just keep doing their thing. Honestly, it was almost comical. I mean at any moment, one of them could've swooped on Jimmy.

But he just keeps on talking, you know? Just part of life. Unfazed. Like ol' Teddy Roosevelt at San Juan Hill. Then BOOM! Like six feet away. And Jimmy just keeps on.

"So he's telling us 'Here's what we need, fellas. Here's what we *neeeeeed*. Ummmm, I dunno (his voice goes up again on that second syllable). Ummmm, you tell me. Is there some way you could deploy your, ummmmm, well, you're supposed to *intelligent*, right? Top of the food chain. I know them ugly birds won't bother you. You think, you think, you *thinnnnnnk* you could keep 'em off us for a few days, while we're all getting ready to move the kids on out of here? Eh? Eh? *Ehhhhhhh?*' To which his chorus responded with an oompa loompa inflected harmony of ehhhhhhhs. And then BOOM! Two more little toads plucked. And no reaction from Jimmy. Part of life. But obviously he knew, and he was hoping we could help him do something about it.

"So Lucius says to him, 'You lets me and Benno noodle that one a bit, Jimmy. We gonna take a little noodlin' walk and tell you if we get a good idea out of it.' Jimmy and his crew replied with around twenty seconds of 'ok, ok, ok, ok, ok, okkkkkkkkkk,' like that, and Lucius and I found some privacy around twenty yards off and started noodlin'.

159

"We paced and we noodled. I said to Lucius, 'Now, that's a real problem they've got there, son. I can't fathom how they just stand there like nothing with them crows dive bombing them every fifteen seconds! Man, it's like a frog Vietnam in there or something. I'm not even a frog, and I'm half traumatized!'

"And Lucius says, 'I know what you mean. Dem frogs is some cool cats!' Well, Lucius got that right, and a nice turn of phrase, to boot. The frogs are cool cats; I told Lucius he'd turned a good one there, which he already knew.

"So we noodled in silence for another minute, and then Lucius comes out with, 'Well...what about yo scarecrows over dere.' He gestured towards our house.

"'My what?' I replied.

"'Yo scarecrows! From way back Halloween when you used to put dem out fo da li'l kids and all.'

"'Okay, Lucius,' I said. 'I remember. Scarecrows. So what we gonna do with those scarecrows?!'

"Well, he shook his head at me like he sometimes did when he thought I was fooling with him, and he answered, 'What we gonna do wid scarecrows? You foolin' wid Lucius, you is. My oh my. What we gonna do wid *scarecrows*? Well, we gonna scare some *crows* is what we gonna do!' And he laughed at my dry sense of humor, which in this case, unfortunately, was totally unintended. Lucius was a step ahead of me. Or I was a step behind me. Either way, once his idea hit me in the face, I got it.

"'Well, I'd say that's a genius idea, Lucius,' I told him. 'One question: you reckon it's safe to go on over to the house? I'm kinda at a maybe on that one. Not sure I'd go over in daylight.'

"And he responded, 'Just like I be thinkin', too. Dat's right. No daytime trip. But we could go in da dark, I bet.'

"'I bet we could. We'd need to be careful. Make sure the neighbors don't see us climbing up outta here. But I bet we could.'

"And he repeated, 'I bet we could, too. Lesgo tell Jimmy and dem we got a plan wid da scarecrows.'

"So that's what we did. The frogs didn't fully grasp the scarecrow concept, but they were willing to suspend doubt and embrace hope. Meantime, the crows kept having their field day there. Getting fat and happy. Another one coming in and then another, at frequent but irregular intervals. Jarringly irregular, with their terrifying screeches of 'Aaw, Aaw!' And then the wingbeats, Mordecai, which were the very sound of death.

"We spent the day down in the swamp, leisurely, circumambulating the pond, venturing back up northward a bit into that woods where we'd passed some time that morning. The sun had arced high above us. It was a clear sky, hardly a cloud. It grew warm but there was plenty of shade from the trees, and we moved in the direction of the river and found a shaded place to sit along the riverbank. There was a nice breeze coming down the river corridor, so between that and the shade and us getting up and dipping our hands in the 'Hooch now and then and pouring it on our heads, we were comfortable. Very comfortable. We had spent many times like this over the years, just a few hundred yards downstream at my house, but of course this felt different. We were only a few hundred yards from home, but it felt like a hundred miles, a hundred years. You know how it is -- the estates across the river are all up on the hill, behind the trees. You can't see them, and they can't see the river. So we were sitting with the trees, and looking across the river at more trees, and the river flowing by. We were upstream at the point where you've got some of those little rapids there, with the small boulders sticking up. So we had the gurgle and whoosh of that, and the soft, easy click-clack of the breeze through the branches and leaves. It was all the familiar sounds. Nothing else. You know the little island just a little up from your place? Well, we watched a full family of deer leap down the bank there, and swim across the river to around thirty yards from where we were setting. I'd caught sight of a deer or two swimming the river before, but only for a few seconds, and never coming more or less right at me. Well, I mean...it was beautiful. They came on up out of the river on our side, shook off, and first one, then all of them caught sight of us. They were their usual alert selves, but we weren't moving anywhere to alarm them, and then Lucius gave them a wheezy 'shhhhi' sound -- that's one of their language's core sounds, like 'shh' with a quick, soft 'ih' sound at the end, or like 'shit' without the t -- he gave them a 'shi,' and then they went about their business. We watched them some more and then turned our eyes back towards the river.

"'You like it here?' Lucius asked.

"'I do," I told him. 'Very much.'

"'Me, too,' he said. And then we both laid back and looked up at the sky through the trees, through the branches and leaves of the trees. Shadyside leaves and sunshot leaves, shadyside branches and sunshot branches. And the big blue up top and over it all.

"And I asked him, 'Remember how you used to talk to the blades of grass when we were kids?'

"'Course I do.' I let out what I'm a little embarrassed to tell you was a small giggle, then Lucius laughed, then I laughed some more, and we were laughing. It was funny because nothing really funny had been said, or had happened. We just started laughing thinking about the old days, when we were kids.

"'Did the grass understand you? I mean, did the blades of grass answer back?' I asked.

"'No. No, dey didn't. That was just fun. Imaginin'. Dem grasses and trees and all don't talk. You can hear 'em, but it's not like talkin', and you don't know if dey *understandin'*.'

"'How 'bout Mister Moon?' I asked, and we both started to laughing again.

"'Mistuh Moon? Now he's my friend. 'Til today, he's my *good* friend. He kin hear me, but only if da night real clear on account of da long distance.'

"'Can you hear him?'

"'No, but I know what he's sayin'.'

"Well, Mordecai, the answer made its own kinda sense, and I took it at that. It was good enough for me. We laughed a little more for no good reason, then just lay there looking up at the sky. Before long, I dozed off.

"I had another dream. Another doozie. Lucius and I were in the river heading downstream. We weren't walking, or even swimming, in the usual sense. We were under water, gliding or swooshing under the river's surface. It's like when you're a kid and you dive down under the surface of a swimming pool and try to hold your breath underwater 'til you get to the other side. Except we weren't exactly swimming a breast stroke or any other stroke for that matter. It felt like we were beavers or river otters swooshing through the water. It was clear in there, a brown green tint but clear, and we could see where we were going and everything around us. You know, as much as they say there's supposed to be good fishing where we are on the river, I'd never actually seen a fish. Never seen one! Well, I tell you what, there are *plenty* of actual fish in there, beauties. Nice stripers just like they say, silver with black stripes. Nice and fat and a couple feet long. And we saw turtles, the ones that never let you get up too close, we passed plenty of those as well. And we saw ducks, first we saw their web feet from underneath, and then we saw them face-to-face when they'd stick their beaks down to snag some little thing or another. And

Mordecai, we were *cruisin'*, all underneath the surface, faster than a kayak riding the current, I'd say. Sleek and fast. And then we discovered in the bottom of the river there were entrances to tunnels, and we dived through them. They were filled with clear water. We could only go through head to foot because otherwise they weren't wide enough to fit. And we'd dive down into them and propel ourselves fifteen, twenty, sometimes forty feet to the exit holes back up into the river and keep swooshing along. And along the banks there were these marvelous root systems from the trees. And the root systems created their own tunnel structures that we could swim through slalom style. All the while, the water rushing over our skin feeling like we were beavers or river otters, all slick and wet, jetting along.

"We kept going. Couple times, just for fun, we broke the surface like dolphins and then angled back down under. And then we angled rightward, towards our bank of the river, and noticed another network of roots. We shot over towards it, and it quickly became clear that, in fact, behind the tangle of roots, it was an underwater cavern. We made our way through that tangle and entered the cavern. It extended deep and far under and into the bank of the river, surely even under our houses. It was a large, clear,

166

underground pool. We raised our heads, over the water and under the earth, and saw that the pool stretched ahead of us indefinitely. Within it, channels had been cut, and we jetted and cut from one channel to another. We couldn't believe how far we were going. We were headed in that downstream direction, and we just kept going and going. Sometimes fish and otters and beavers would swoosh past us going in the opposite direction, and we'd feel their skins against ours for that split-second as we passed. *Finally*, all at once and at high speed, we both shot up through an exit hole into the creek that separates the polo fields from Schiffer's property. Just in the cavern, we'd probably covered seven or eight hundred yards -- under the end of our neighborhood, under Arnaud's property, under the entire polo fields. We looked around and saw where we were. And then we looked at each other and started laughing like kids. Joyful laughing.

"I woke up with Lucius nudging me, asking what I was laughing about. I told him I'd just dreamed we lived in the river like fish or otters, and the river let off into a huge underground swimming pool under Arnaud's and the polo fields, and we'd just swum all the way through and had a helluva good time. He looked at me and offered how I 'musta been bit by one of dem crazy bugs while I was sleepin'.' I allowed he could be right, we laughed some more, and then headed back to the swamp to get ready for the scarecrow expedition.

"Upon our return, all was as we left it. Crows nabbing frogs, frogs zapping flies, occasional larger critters passing through for a snack or just on their way from the woods over to Arnaud's or the river or somewhere else. Jimmy and his crew reacted immediately to our return with a chorus of 'hey, hey, heys' and a general look of relief. They probably considered us a flight risk; in any event, we were the crux of their latest survival plan, so they were happy to see us again.

"We passed the afternoon in what seemed to be typical swamp fashion, just hanging around, not doing much. Of course, the locals were ever ready and opportunistic feeders, so that kept most of them busy much of the day. It occurred to me at some point that afternoon that we hadn't eaten or had anything to drink for going on a day, and though I didn't feel especially weak, which was surprising, the realization gave me pause. I mentioned in passing to Lucius that we might grab us a little snackeroo when we went by the house that night for the scarecrows, and he agreed. He said if I was real hungry, he could grab me a frog to eat any time.

He said if I took a real strong bite down on the neck right away and killed it, it wouldn't wiggle all the way down, and it might tide me over. I told him I appreciated that bit of swamp wisdom, but I just as soon wait and raid the ice box later on.

"So there we were, Mordecai, minding our own business, and along comes a big 'ol Eastern River Cooter, those turtles you see sunning themselves on logs in the river. Well, I was surprised to see him approach us because I know how shy they are. But there he was. From the size of him, I'd say he was twenty years old at least. Big. Probably a few inches more than a foot long and right about a foot wide. Not too tall, not that turtles are ever too tall, but probably the top of his shell wasn't more than four or five inches off the ground.

"Well, he crawls right up to us and says something, and then Lucius says something, and then I grab Lucius's hand.

"'What's your name, turtle?' Lucius asked him.

"'Scooter' he said. I don't know if he knew his official species name, but I got a kick out of that one, Mordecai. Scooter the Cooter. Well, Lucius told him our names and asked him why he come over. 'It's a long story,' he started. Funny how in the swamp when someone starts off telling you it's a long story, you kinda perk up. Usually, I'd pretty much tune out right then and there.

"So Lucius says, 'We got time, Scooter. Go on and tell.'

"'All right. Thanks,' he said. He had a kind of low, mournful tone to his voice. I hadn't spoken with other turtles before, so I don't know if that's just how they sound or if Scooter was a particular depressive. Either way, the sound of his voice was a welcome balance to the sharp 'Aw, Aws' of the crows and the other high-pitched chirps going on all around us. 'Here's my problem,' he went on. 'My wife, Beth, well -- I told her we'd have this problem but she wouldn't listen. So what she did is, she put all our eggs over here (he gestured with his neck somewhere off to the left), in a pile of leaves near the pond. I mean, it's a nice spot and all, I get it, nice coverage, safe. But it's way the heck over here, and we really should be over there (neck gesture towards the river). That's where we all are, our whole group. There's plenty of plant stuff to eat there, nice logs, and the water's deeper so we can really get down out of danger if we need to, which happens a lot, like every few minutes. So we've got to get over there. The kids hatched a few days ago, and they're okay so far, but it's dangerous here. And this is the part I was really mad at Beth about, but, you know, she wouldn't listen -- we need to get across the road and across one big yard to get to the river. And the babies are really slow. I mean they barely walk, and they just started to see this morning. Between cars running them -- us -- over, and someone eating them while we're wide open there on someone's lawn, I mean something bad's bound to happen. I'm kinda stressed about it to be honest. And Beth won't admit that I warned her, and she's pretty much not talking to me now. Anyhow, we should really try to make it to the river. Could you help?'

"'We could try,' Lucius said. 'What would help?'

"'Oh, man, you guys are the best,' he said, still sounding depressed. 'Yeah. So what you could do is kinda walk with us across the road and across someone's lawn so no one kills us on the way over to the river.'

"So Lucius asked him, 'Well, how long you expect it gonna take you to get on over to da river?'

"'Well, we're turtles. So I guess you'd have to factor that in. Um...um.......um..........a while. It'll take a while,' Scooter answered. Our dilemma was that we didn't want to stir up the humans in the neighborhood with the site of our bedraggled selves out and about. And the longer we were gonna be exposed, the higher the odds of someone seeing us. On the other hand, Scooter seemed like a good turtle; it wasn't his idea that led them to their current predicament. And, oh, what the hell. So we told him we'd help.

"'But Lucius, tell him it's gonna be *real* late night, early morning when they'll need to be ready,' I said. I wanted to reduce the chances of being seen as much as we could. Lucius told him, he agreed, and we had another good deed on our hands. I wouldn't have guessed, Mordecai, that swamp life would lead to so much do-gooding."

'Well, there you go,' I said to Benno.

"'Well, there you go' -- very helpful analysis, Mordecai. Very helpful. If you ever think about going into the color commentator business, think again. Good grief.' He winked at me and continued.

"So that night, probably around one-thirty in the morning, we gave Scooter a thirty-minute warning to get his troops ready for the big move. Though they were all within around forty-five feet of us, we knew they could use the time. Two o'clock rolls around, and we're all ready. It was me, Lucius, Scooter, his wife (a lovely turtle lady, by the way) and nineteen of the most adorable little baby Cooters you've ever seen. Like little brown-green pancakes with heads. Clumsy crawlers, but determined.

"So we set out. We decided best to come out of the swamp on the south, or downstream side, which is closest to my house, so there'd be less space over which we'd all be exposed. We'd herd them over to my house and around to the backyard. Once we got there, at least Lucius and I would be safe we figured. And we'd usher them right to the river's edge, and then go into the garage and look for the scarecrows. We started, and it probably took five or ten minutes to get from the edge of the swamp up that incline to the road. The little hill there slowed their slowness down even more, and there was so much brush and branches and leaves that Scooter and Mrs. Scooter had their hands full keeping track of everyone. But eventually they all made it up and we started to make our way across the major thoroughfare known to you and me, Mordecai, as Deerfield Drive. Twenty feet across. Took us probably three minutes. Thank goodness, no cars came by because neither Lucius nor I really knew what we'd do if they had. Anyway, we got across and headed towards my front yard. Another forty feet, another seven minutes or so. Once they hit the level grass, they got a little faster. Better traction I think. We were on the move. Around to the back of the house we went. Now, Mordecai, I don't want to toot my own horn, or Lucius's horn, but in my backyard we encountered two handsomely sized racoons. They would've feasted on a few of the children -- I know that for a fact -- and maybe even Mr. and Mrs. Scooter. But me and Lucius, we run them off. Man, was Scooter ever grateful. Couldn't stop thanking us. He still *sounded* depressed, but 'thank you, thank you, thank you!' he kept saying. The whole slow-moving, sad-sack group of them couldn't have been happier. We got them to the river over the two hundred fifty feet or so length of my backyard (twenty more minutes), and in they went. Those little pancake-looking baby turtles -- they were something -- crawling and falling down the river bank and plop, right in the river, and then *right away* swimming. They knew exactly what to do. One more meaningful, sad look from the joyful Scooter, and off he and the Missus went as well. I tell you what, Mordecai -- Lucius and I looked at each other, and we felt *good*.

"We headed to the backdoor of my house, got the hidden key out from the spot we kept it on the porch, and opened the side door to the garage. I flipped the lights on, and, sure enough, there were the scarecrows, pretty much in plain sight though I don't think I'd noticed them there for many years. And there were *four* of them. Jimmy and Marty and the crew would be very pleased assuming the plan worked and the scarecrows kept the crows and other birds away. We picked up the scarecrows, carried them out the garage, and propped them up against the side of the house. It was time for our snackeroo, so I took the key, opened the backdoor, and in we went. Back in the old kitchen. There was my easy chair and the couch and the little TV I watched during breakfast. There was the fridge and pantry. There was the kitchen table. There was the pallet Lucius used on the floor, his favorite. It had only been a day, a day and a half, since we took our canoe trip that had kicked this all off. I asked Lucius if he could believe it had just been a day.

"'No *way* I don't,' he replied. 'Lucius and Benno been *out* dere in da world for *real.*'

"'Yes, we have, Lucius. Yes, we have,' I said. I was actually in a state of shock at the thought. I moved absently around the kitchen, opened the refrigerator door, looked in, closed it; walked in the pantry, looked around, walked out; opened the fridge once more.

"'Any Coca Cola in there?' Lucius asked hopefully. That got me out of my daze, and back to remembering that I was hungry and thirsty and that's what we were doing inside the house in the first place. I poured us each a Coke, made us each a turkey sandwich with mayo and mustard, grabbed us each a half sour pickle, and we started to eat, me at the table, Lucius in his usual spot on the floor, opposite me, his back against the cabinet that held our pots and pans. I was back deep in my thoughts. Probably a couple minutes went by before Lucius asked me if I reckoned it was safe for us to come back and live in the house again.

"Well, I was in one of those places where your mind kinda strikes glancing blows at a whole bunch of thoughts one after the other but never really bears down on just one of them. And the idea Lucius had just mentioned -- that was one of those ideas I had glancing around in there. 'Probably is, Lucius. None of those Klan boys or whatever they are showed up last night, and none showed up so far tonight or earlier today. So yeah, probably is safe.'

"'You wants to come back in here den, suh?' he asked.

"'Strangely, son, I don't. Not quite yet. How 'bout you?'

"He smiled at me and said, 'You da boss, sir. You know *dat*. But even so and all, I'm just fine stayin' out a little more. You can always count on Lucius for mo' expeditionin'.

"'And Lucius can always count on ol' Benno for a little more expeditionin' as well,' I said, and we both laughed. Lucius got up, and I did also. I gave him a clap on the shoulder; he smiled and gave me a clap on mine; we threw out our garbage, collected the scarecrows, and carried them back down to the swamp, side by side, each of us with a scarecrow under each arm.

"Mordecai, there might have been a thousand frogs and toads there in the swamp watching us descend the little hill and re-enter their amphibian kingdom, each one I'd say looking at us with great hope -- great hope. Like warriors home from a successful mission, we simply walked on by. We were tired. We found a place to bed down, and I actually had the idea of using the scarecrows as pillows. So we did that, me and Lucius. A good number of the frogs had followed us, and I'm sure they had *no* earthly idea what we were doing using these magical creatures we had returned with as pillows or whatever they thought we were doing with them. I said something to Lucius about that, we had a conspiratorial kinda chuckle between us, put our heads down on the scarecrows, and man, we fell asleep just like that. Out fast and out deep.

"In the morning, we woke up just before first light, but it was light enough to see that all around us, in a kind of flat level amphitheater arrangement, every single one of the frogs and toads old enough to have an interest in this historic moment in their lives was waiting on us expectantly. I opened my eyes, propped myself up on one elbow, and as if on cue, all the frogs and toads cocked their head to the side, all, remarkably, to the same side, in the fashion we'd seen Jimmy look at us the day before. It was clear it was time for us to get up and post these wondrous and brave miracles made of straw out in the pond part of the swamp. So up we stood, and we gathered the scarecrows, each of us again with one under each of our arms. Without a word, we marched out into the pond. Now, Mordecai, as I had to occasionally remind myself, I'd only been a creature of the wild for one full day and a part of a second day. If you had told me two days before that I would be walking into that murk of a swamp under any circumstances, I'd have told you you were crazy. And in fact, as we took our first steps from the damp, leafy edge of the pond into the shallow and dark murk itself, I was a bit uneasy. You never know what's under the water. But Lucius seemed fully at ease, and I had cottoned enough to the notion of myself as a wilderness survivalist that after a step or two I was just fine.

"The posts attached to the bottom of the scarecrows were not that long, so we couldn't stake them down too far out into the middle of the pond. So we waded in up to around knee height, and Lucius and I stabbed them down into the bottom in four spots, each around twenty feet from the other, roughly in a square. As we climbed out of the pond, Jimmy and the extended crew looked at us as though to say, 'that's all'?   And, in fact, the first thing Lucius said to them once we were on dry land was 'That's all.'

"Even though we had described to them already and in repetitive detail to satisfy their skepticism and curiosity, exactly how and why the scarecrows were going to work, they remained a dubious congregation. There was nothing to do but wait and see, which is exactly what we all proceeded to do. After around ten or fifteen minutes, a first little squadron of crows could be heard approaching from the distance. The frogs and toads were waiting, tense. The crows came into sight, started their descent, pulled up, circled, looked, let out a frustrated sounding chorus of 'Aw, Aws,' and flew away. There was a cautiously optimistic outburst of chirp-croaks all around us. We heard another group of crows approaching, and the same sequence of events occurred. At this point our friends were convinced, and they burst out into a great frenzy of elation. Chirp-croaks, moo-croaks, and everything in between. And soon enough, the celebratory chant of 'Lucius and Benno, Lucius and Benno' broke out once more.

"Mordecai, a piece of advice my daddy gave me that I always remembered, maybe the *only* piece, is that you always want to

'Leave 'em smiling.' That's what he said, 'Leave 'em smiling.' Well, Lucius and I, if I do say so myself, had done a bang-up job for these little frogs and toads. There wasn't much room for us to go up in their estimation after that, so in my view it was time to leave 'em smiling and move on. I looked at Lucius and said, 'Lucius, my boy, I do believe our work here is done.'

"'Yessuh, Benno. I believe you right,' he answered. 'Where you thinkin' we ought to go next?'

"Well, I had a very specific idea, and I said to him, 'You know, Lucius, I had a dream couple nights ago in that parking lot that I was running with a herd of deer. Beautiful bucks they were. I'd kinda like to meet some of them. I've always wondered what their lives are like.'

"'We can *sho' enough* do that,' Lucius said with a big smile. "Dem bucks and I, and dem does, too -- we goes *way* back.'

"And I knew they did. Because like I said before, Lucius went way back with *all* of 'em."

One of the aides came outside and told Benno it was time for dinner. He'd been on a roll since right after lunch. I started saying how I'd be seeing him the following week, but Benno would have none of it.

"Next week?!" he said. "No, sir. No sir, Mordecai. You c'mon in with me for dinner. I'm too close to the end to stop and wait another week."

Of course, I obliged his request. I stayed for dinner and then on into the evening until he finished his remarkable story.

Part Three - The Fields

Chapter 9

"You might wonder, Mordecai, as I sometimes did, whether there was some single congregation point for all the deer we see around the neighborhood. I've also wondered how many there are. Am I just seeing the same groups of three or four or five deer all the time? I really had no idea."

We had been served dinner, sat down, and that's how Benno started in. He was on a roll, and he was going to keep on rolling. There were a few other residents at our table, and the ones who could hear listened. The ones who couldn't alternated between smiling, frowning, and squinting. It's neither here nor there, but it's an odd human instinct to squint when we can't hear something. I've never understood that, but as I say, it's neither here nor there. As Benno continued his story to its conclusion over the course of that evening, a few more residents gathered around to listen. While many of them were familiar with the premise of his story, I got the clear sense that no one had heard it through anywhere near to the end. And evidently, for those who gathered, Benno presented better programming that evening then whatever else the Home was offering. He was aware of his audience but not altered by it. His manner of relating these events continued as before -- animated and totally unselfconscious.

"Well, I was with Lucius," he continued. "And when you're with Lucius, what you do is go sit somewhere in the woods, or you might walk around here or there, and you basically just wait for a deer or a herd of them to materialize. Aside from being in the woods, it's not that much different from how we end up seeing the deer in the neighborhood under the usual circumstances. You know what I mean? They just pop up, crossing the street, or eating grass in your backyard, or climbing up out of the swamp or the river. They just appear.

"It's funny, Mordecai, but as you know, my house was flush up against Arnaud's property. I wouldn't say that Arnaud was my neighbor because all you'd ever see of him was the fence he put up and the no trespassing signs on the fence. But I *would* say that his *property* was my neighbor. And you don't have to be a zoologist or whatever you call it to notice the frequent traveling of deer from the

Arnaud property over onto my lawn and then continuing towards and past yours. The deer don't have to observe the no trespassing signs, but we do. They've got the better of us on that one, I suppose. In any event, as you also know, they go wherever they want. I was always happy to see them crossing over into my backyard, and I always wondered where they were going and what they were up to. I mean, I know they're looking to eat, but when they're not eating I always wondered if there was anything else special they did. And I always kind of figured that at least some of them call Arnaud's property their home. Since he put that fence up all around his land ten or fifteen years ago, they're protected in there, at least from humans. I know it sounds a little silly, but for a long time, I considered the Dwyers to be my neighbors to the left -- as you're looking at the river -- and the deer to be my neighbors to the right. And the way it is in neighborhoods these days, I probably saw more of the deer than the Dwyers."

Benno allowed himself a little chuckle at that social observation, but of course he was right. You might see adult neighbors out and about with regularity when their kids were young, but after that, not so much. I don't say that with any attitude of judgement or criticism; I fit the pattern myself. But the odd result is that in a neighborhood of humans -- God's most complex and fully developed creatures -- the deer are the most interesting neighbors.

"So I told Lucius that I'd love to get on over onto Arnaud's property somehow and wait around and see what we'd see. We had been in the swamp and the woods long enough. It was lovely, much of it, but my curiosity on that score was satisfied. And I liked the idea of finally making inroads onto 'ol Arnaud's property. And I probably also liked the idea, to be truthful, of knowing we were right next door to home. Even if we spent another night or two out on the move, it was good to know home was there.

"To get to Arnaud's property was a challenge. It was fenced off on the side bordering my property, and the next nearest point of potential access was from the river. We first walked along the fence line to see if there was an opening we could get through, but there wasn't. So back down into the river we went, right where we started two days earlier. You can have days when nothing happens that feel like forever, and you can have days when everything happens that pass in a flash. The feeling I got going back down into the river with Lucius was actually neither of these precisely. It was remarkable to think how little time had passed. And it's true that for the entirety of those two days, time seemed to fly. At the same time, it felt like my world had turned upside down, which isn't something you can measure by a number of hours or events. It was something else.

"We slogged along through the river mud trying as best we could to stay to the areas that looked driest. But the Chattahoochee bottom has its special suck, and there's no way to cleanly pass through it. So slog we did, and slow-going it was. A couple times we saw deer tracks on the edge of the river and climbing up the bank, but not being deer we didn't venture those. They were too steep. After around a hundred yards we found some tracks going up an embankment that we could handle, and we climbed up out of the mess. We were still sporting our natty outfits of swim trunks and aqua socks, and the last two days had left us pretty well dirtied up. So the new layer of river mud covering us up to our knees didn't make a noticeable difference in our appearance, not that anyone was looking.

"If you've spent any time, Mordecai, looking over the fence at Arnaud's property, you know that grove there is really beautiful. Even if you hadn't entered the kind of Neverland which I had, it would look to you like a setting for fairy tales. The trees were planted decades ago in twenty long, loosely measured rows, and cover an area a hundred yards by a hundred yards. The section bordering the river was planted with Georgia Pines, and the section to its right as you looked over the fence, bordering the rest of the field, was all hard woods -- great, arching, mature trees. Beneath them was a downy undergrowth of overgrown grass and weeds fluffing up probably a foot high. And along the fence line and then between the two sections of trees, a gravel road ran to the far side of the property and around the perimeter. Beyond the trees and to the right, was open meadow, and a pond, and further to the right, one of the power lines cut through from our neighborhood on over to the polo fields and past. It was on the grassy ground, in the grove, that we sat and propped ourselves up against a tree, Lucius against one side and me clockwise around against the next.

"Well, we waited and waited. I had some level of confidence that the deer would show up. One time Jack Dwyer told me that he would often walk past my house to the fence of the property at night and shine a bright flashlight over in the direction where we had posted ourselves, and more often than not he would see a whole bunch of deer eyes light up, looking right back at him, frozen by the light. He said they bedded down in there, and it made sense to me given how protected and comfortable it was. That knowledge, combined with Lucius's instinct that the way to go about this was just to pick a spot and wait, made me feel comfortable that we were doing what we could do to facilitate the meeting.

"So we continued to wait, and eventually daytime faded, and the night opened up. Turned out it was a full moon that night, and a blood moon at that. The moon glowed like it was Mars. And just as the morning sunshine had slanted into the swamp, the moon's tinted light fell through the trees all around us.

"I said to Lucius, 'Looks like Mister Moon's angry tonight.' But instead of responding, he reached his right arm around the bend of the tree and motioned me to be silent. He had turned his head forty-five degrees in the opposite direction, so I leaned forward slightly to see what he was looking at. And behold, Mordecai, it was a herd of five bucks. Their tan skins were russet in the moonlight. The bucks and the does have their own herds most of the year. The does and the fawns herd together, and the bucks herd together. And there's always an alpha buck, and at that very moment he was standing at the head of the herd looking right at us. We were sitting down which added to the impression of his size, but I would say he was four feet tall at the shoulders, and six feet at the top of his rack which was a magnificent ten-pointer.

"He was looking down at us, silent and lordly, and then Lucius began to speak. He spoke in that 'shi' sounding language I described to you the other day. At least some of the sounds sounded like that. I reached around and took his hand so I could understand what they were saying. But almost as soon as I did, they stopped talking. The alpha buck stared at me, not in the quizzical way that Jimmy and the frogs had in the swamp, but with full composure, his eyes still and unblinking, his body planted and calm. It was strange; I was almost nervous, but not; almost confused, but not. I looked at Lucius, and, like the buck, he just looked back at me. Somehow I knew they were waiting for me to say something. So I said the only thing I knew to say, 'shi'! They both let out a laugh, the buck said, 'Come on!' and then we were off. The seven of us, running through the trees and into the open on Arnaud's property. And as I fell into stride, it hit me right away -- this is my dream. The dream from our first night out, from the parking lot -- it was happening! Mind you, we weren't naked in the real version; we still had our trunks on. But it was the dream realized -- being with the deer, the feeling of freeness and flight. And again like the dream, the awareness of a song, a soundless song, like my heart was singing. And the sense of speed and strength beyond anything I'd ever known. And the feeling of being young, even younger than I ever was as we dashed and leapt across Arnaud's field."

As he told this last part of the story, his physical mannerisms, his conducting, became wider open and totally fluid, gestural, graceful, as though he were painting a house in some new, unbounded manner. And parts of the story started to sound almost like recitations -- things he had told himself again and again like articles of faith. I could picture him, as the concerned neighbors must have, sitting by the river and proclaiming without and within these utterances like prayers.

He continued in more prosaic style. "It was something, Mordecai. Really something. We finished this first burst by leaping the fence between Arnaud's property and the polo fields. The bucks stopped at that point, sniffed around for a second, and commenced feeding on the grass and shrubs bordering the woods that surrounded the fields. I think you know, Mordecai, but for my friends here (he referred to the six or seven residents of the Home who had gathered around), where we leapt the fence to the polo fields was at the point where the actual large polo field is. So looking from that vantage point, you'd look down the full length of the field, with around fifty yards of border at each end, so around two hundred sixty yards. To your left, you've got around eighty yards of woods bordering part of the side of the field. That's where the herd was feeding just then. And then past that to the left opens up to a smaller, probably half-size, practice field. And then to the left of that you have some fenced off pasture for grazing the horses that's around the same size as the practice field. Then, to the left of that, you've got a walking path and then the river. Now, looking straight ahead from where we crossed, you've got the full length of the field plus some buffer, and then you've got the creek separating the fields from the Schiffer property. The creek, and then he has a fence up as well. And finally, to the right, you've got the sheds where they run the polo operations out of, with some long runners strung between posts that the ponies can be hooked on to while they're waiting their turn, and then both behind that and past it, you've got beautiful, wide open grazing areas for the horses. Long grass, shade trees -- whatever a horse could want. All fenced in but plenty of room.

"So the deer were eating grass, and Lucius and I were pretty much standing there watching the show. It felt a little awkward, almost rude, that we weren't eating with them as they'd clearly invited us along. But whatever magical thing had just happened, we still had the same digestive systems we'd had a few days before, and damn sure we weren't gonna start stuffing grass and shrubbery down our gullets. So we watched, and I took the opportunity to ask Lucius what he and the alpha had said to each other.

"He answered, 'Oh, he was just askin' why I was wid you, and if you was okay and all. And dats right when you said "shi!" Dat was some good timin' from 'Ol Benno.'

"'Well, look at me' I said. 'Developing animal instincts of my own.' And we both laughed.

"Meantime, the herd started to migrate across the polo field towards one of the fenced in grazing areas where around ten of the brown, beautiful horses were. It seemed like we were edging over there in an absent minded, non-intentional kind of way, but once we got there, the bucks started getting on the horses' case. Trash-talking them. That's an expression, right? 'Trash-talking.'"

"Yes," I told him.

"I thought so. And now this part requires a little explanation. The horses and the deer have a not-so-friendly rivalry. I mean, no one gets hurt. Nothing like that. It's more like color wars at camp, like they're on opposing teams and like to prank or tease each other. And here's the really interesting thing because it never would have occurred to me. Primarily, the deer get on the horses for not busting out of their paddocks and living the free life like the deer do. Those horses, I mean, they're just grand animals. In Lucius's evolution system, they rank real high, higher than the deer. They could bust through those fences or even jump over them whenever they wanted to. But as a rule they don't. And why? Well, they've made a conscious deal with themselves to give that up in exchange for a pretty cushy life there. They've got all the food and water they need right at their disposal; they've got protection from the elements as necessary; and they've got medical help if they need it. For all that, they don't mind staying where they are, respecting their boundaries, letting people ride them. If you think of it, it's not a bad deal at all. And they're kept clean and beautiful to boot, which they don't mind either.

"The deer, on the other hand, and particularly these cheeky bucks, think the horses are a bunch of pansy asses who traded their freedom for a soft life. So the bucks like to flaunt their *own* freedom. They get right up by the paddocks and trash talk the horses -- with glee; they love it. The horses, on the other hand, they think their shit smells sweet. They know they're bigger and stronger than the deer, and though it's close, they know they can run faster if they need to. The deer are better jumpers, but that's about all the horses will give them. They won't concede anything else. They try to ignore the deer. They'll tell them stuff like, 'Yeah, you *wish* you were more useful so you even had the *chance* to live like us. Maybe if you could actually do something anyone *cared* about, people would be interested in something other than shooting you!'

"So there we were in that red moonlight, with our herd, listening but trying not to get drawn into the back and forth. And as if on cue, the bucks all at once leapt the paddock fence into the horses' enclosure and sprinted and sprung this way and that. The area was two hundred yards long and a hundred yards wide, dotted with trees and bordered on the far side by woods, so there was plenty of room. Lucius and I looked at each other but thought better of leaping in ourselves. You could clearly sense it wasn't the first time the bucks had done this, and the horses, by their reaction, were clearly annoyed. They started up with a clamor of neighing and foot stomping and taking little charges at the deer who would zag and zig out of the way. It was an interesting dynamic because you could tell that the horses didn't want to let on that they were too annoyed, and yet it was annoying. In particular, the bucks, when they got to a safe distance, would start nibbling the long sweet grass growing inside the fences. Well, that was the horses' bread and butter, so to speak, and they'd charge at the bucks in earnest. After a couple of charges like this, the bucks, again in unison and as if on cue, beat a long-strided exit towards the fencing, leapt it, and we were able to rejoin them.

"'Why didn't you come?' the alpha asked.

"'We just visitin' is all,' Lucius answered. 'My friend here (he nodded towards me), he never been a deer. He still figurin' it out.'

"'Weak-ass horses,' was the alpha's response. And we made our way -- bounding and leaping -- back to the where we started with them, which, as Jack Dwyer had once told me, was one of the places where they bedded down.

"It's an unusual experience bedding down with deer. They sleep mostly with their eyes open. So it's hard to tell for sure whether a particular deer is asleep. And even when they are, they don't stay asleep for much more than thirty seconds at a time before lifting their heads up for a quick look about. And then every thirty minutes or so, they're liable to stand up, pee, and look around some more. They sleep only as much as they absolutely need to. They spend a lot of time bedded down, but very little of that time are they actually asleep. Lucius and I lay down that night knowing we would be well guarded.

"As we lay there, my mind kept returning to the back and forth between the bucks and the horses. It was obvious, though it never occurred to me, that the horses could all bust out of their fences and go free pretty much any time they wanted. And I could see the bucks' point; it was thrilling and kind of glorious to live with their kind of freedom. *Out there*, you know? I say this as a human, a free human with a perch on top of the food chain: their freedom seemed freer. At the same time, the life of the horses seemed more familiar to me. I could personally relate to it more easily. Steady meals, regular and controlled interactions with the same cast of characters day in and day out, staying in the same prescribed area -- it felt more like my life. And it made me think about my life -- the fact that my life felt to me more like the lives of horses who lived inside of a fenced-in paddock. That's quite a thought to absorb. And compared to most people, I knew I had very little exerting a hold on me. I didn't have a wife or kids. I didn't need to work for a living. I even had my good health. I could be traveling, on the move.

Even so, even with all of this, especially with all of this, it was strange to feel there was a level of freedom somehow beyond mine.

"And then I thought about Lucius. I wondered what he made of the tit for tat earlier that night. He was a slave, but he and I pretty much had the same life. It was hard to wrap my mind around that. I wasn't sure what it meant one way or another. I suppose it meant that he was also more like the horses than the bucks. Then it occurred to me that like the horses he could pretty much run away anytime he wanted. Hell, he could walk away. What was I going to do, chase him? That thought scared me because he was all I had. What would I do with myself day after day without Lucius? Who would I talk to? Who would I eat with?

"But then I thought, what if he wanted to go? What if he was a horse that saw the bucks every day and had secretly wanted to be one for all these years? Well, that thought made me sad. I was scared at the thought of him leaving and sad at the thought of him staying because he thought he had to.

"And so it was with trepidation that I asked him who he thought had it better, the horses or the deer.

"He gave a chuckle or two and then told me 'Both. Most all da time a horse is happiest bein' a horse, and a deer is happiest bein' a deer.'

"Well, that made me feel a little better because if Lucius and I were both horses, so to speak, then, like me, he was most likely content to remain one. Which was a relief, but didn't feel like it exactly hit the point. So I said, 'You know I wouldn't want to keep you if you wanted to go, right? I don't know what I'd do without you, Lucius, but tell me if you want to go free.'

"And this is what he said to me. He said, 'Don't worry, Benno. I been free pretty much all along. I just didn't want to tell you.'

"Mordecai, I can't tell you all I felt at that moment. It wasn't the answer I expected, and I'm not sure I fully understand it to this day. But it brought such a flood of feeling. Like a dam had broken. I actually started to weep. Our friends the bucks looked over with their steady eyes. Lucius told them it was okay.

"Under that blood moon I took Lucius's hand. 'My brother,' I said. And he said, 'My brother.'"

"The next morning Lucius died with a tick and a thud. As we had the previous morning, we rose and were on the move before first light. The end of night sky was clear -- the red gone, the black fading. Again, as one and at once, we set out. I'd say we spent a good twenty minutes or half an hour eating Arnaud's grass in the field next to the grove -- or our buck friends did. Lucius and I just soaked it in, silent but for our breathing, feet and ankles wet from the morning dew. When real morning came, it was clear and pale blue. We doubled back through the grove towards the river and then turned upstream, first hurdling the fence into my yard, then Dwyer's, then yours and Luke Simpson's, and then into the woods behind the Nolans. As I tried to describe before, it was something remarkable to be so completely with those bucks, so completely out there, in the wild, and at the same time not be more than fifty or sixty paces from my backdoor. We stopped briefly in each of the yards, sniffed around, the bucks nibbled some, peed, shat, and we'd move on. After the Nolan woods, we turned left, trotted past the right side of his house, crossed Deerfield Drive, and went down into the swamp. Our old friends there called out greetings as we went by, but we were moving with the herd and kept moving. We headed north, in an upstream direction into the woods, and then turned left, cutting through the woods behind the two houses there before emerging out into the Georgia Power right of way, under the power lines. The bucks sniffed, ate, and relieved themselves there as well. Now the sun was high enough to start showing above the houses and the trees by the river. We turned and moved again southward, down the right of way, through the long morning shadows, back across the main part of Deerfield, and leapt the fence back into Arnaud's pasture. We were running then, and kept running, across the couple hundred yards and over the next fence onto the polo fields. We paused together, kind of reconnoitered, and then advanced towards the same paddock we'd tormented the previous evening. We leapt in. This time Lucius and I felt comfortable enough with the routine to join them, and we kind of preened and pranced circles around and near the horses, a safe enough distance away to give us a jump on them if and when they charged us, which they did. Again, like the night before, there was a loudness of hoof stomping and neighing. The bucks commenced their grazing tease, snagging mouthfuls of long, sweet grass, looking at the horses while they did it, then marking territory. The great, brown horses grew in anger. 'Sorry-asses!' shouted the bucks, and as a few of them peed, the two biggest of the horses charged right at us. We jumped back and were close enough to the paddock fence that our natural next move was to leap over it back onto the polo fields, which we did. But the two horses leapt the fence right after us, not twenty yards behind. Something between alarm and almost an ecstasy swept the herd. The hair on their backs stood up, and they let out a fervid round of 'shi's.' A chase was on. I was not pleased to be amongst the chased, but the bucks still seemed confident in their skills of evasion, and Lucius seemed okay, and of course, there was nothing for me to do but run with the herd anyway, which I did. Strides twenty feet long, darting, sprinting, cutting, we headed across that first polo field, the full one, towards the river, then cut left back towards Arnaud's, but the two great horses somehow anticipated us and had that angle cut off. So we cut hard to the right, towards Schiffer's. We leapt the creek at the end of the polo fields, took one stride, then leapt the fence onto Schiffer's property. The horses pulled up short of the creek. Whoa, but that was a high, Mordecai. My adrenaline was surging. The herd was celebrating, shouting some last, and safe, insults back over the fence at the horses. Lucius and I were both in a full sweat. We stood there smiling at each other, catching our breath.

"The herd trotted ten yards farther on to Schiffer's property and commenced the usual routine. His house was way up on a hill to our right looking down on the yard and then the river. I'd never been there. It was a nice property. Our herd started to move again, across that yard, farther downstream. Schiffer had let his grass grow long. Maybe some of the horses he owned grazed there sometimes. We were moving easily over the grass when I heard the first tick and thud. Two feet away I saw an arrow, the kind you shoot from a crossbow, lodged deep in the ground. The herd made a break, first one way, then back the other, out of sorts. I heard a second tick, felt the air move right near me, then a second thud, and then a third. These thuds were different -- a fuller, kind of wet sound as they struck. I saw the alpha buck drop in front of me. The rest of us turned hard towards the river. As we did so, I instinctively turned towards Lucius in my fear. And it was then that I realized he wasn't next to me. I stopped. The herd continued to the river. I saw the alpha down bleeding, and then I saw Lucius. He was on his knees. I went back to him. The arrow had hit him on a downward trajectory through the bottom of his neck down into his upper chest. From his knees, he fell full to the ground and lay on his side in the long grass. I knelt by him. 'Hang in there,

Lucius,' I said, and I took his hand. 'Just hang in there. It'll be all right.' He looked me in the eye and opened his mouth, but he couldn't talk. Blood poured out in a stream from the right side of his mouth to the grass, to the ground. I leaned close to him, my left cheek next to his, and hugged him to me. 'I love you,' I told him. 'I loved you our whole life.' He looked at me, closed his eyes in a long blink, opened them, looked at me again, shivered, and was gone. Almost immediately I felt a sharp pain in the middle of my stomach, like my guts were draining out, so painful that I rolled on my side next to him. When after a moment it passed, I sat up, swept a hand over his eyes to close them, kissed him on the forehead, got up, and did my best to run off towards the river. At the end of Schiffer's yard before the river, he had a wooden bridge crossing back over to the polo fields. I crossed it and walked the riverside footpath the length of those fields. Out of nowhere, a young boy appeared, probably ten years old. He showed me a secret way around the end of the fence onto Arnaud's property, and then walked with me the length of the grove where we'd bedded the night before. He helped me cross over into my yard, and then he left. I sat down on my lawn and cried.

"Odd to say, but one of the first things I thought was that it was legal. Schiffer had the right. We were deer, and he was allowed to hunt us. You're not allowed to use a gun to hunt around here, near the city; that would be illegal. But a crossbow is fine. So it was all legal."

Benno let out a sigh. There was sweat on his forehead, and he took out a handkerchief and wiped it off. Of the residents who had joined to listen, some were softly crying, some looked at Benno and then down into their laps. Benno was flushed, and also looked purged, like he'd had a workout. He wiped the sweat from his brow again as an aide led him away.

Chapter 10

Except for a little more, that's Benno's story, and the story of Lucius, his slave.

What can I say, in the end, about Benno? He lived some chunk of his life in a thought world of his own making. That world centered on a relationship long since deemed illegal, and immoral. Yet he filled the world he made with a love for Lucius, which he imagined to be reciprocal. If Lucius wasn't real in our world, and if Benno loved him and was loved by him in the only world in which the friendship lived, well, it's hard for me to get upset. For me, getting mad at Benno is like getting mad at the wind. Benno kept Lucius for a reason, even if he couldn't ever know what that was. My guess is that some way, somehow, it kept him centered and moving forward. We're all looking for something like that. The idea served him.

And clearly, Benno's story serves me as well because I keep wanting to tell it. Some friends have wondered about this, particularly considering the golden light Benno casts on his relationship with someone he believes he owned. Because my conscience is clear, I've felt free to ask myself this question as well. Why do I invest my heart in Benno's story? Is it because I was almost his neighbor and have literally walked the pathways and floated the waterways of his story? Is it because we are both loners by circumstance and maybe by nature? Is it because of my intuition that we are all, in the end, only children, regardless of age, regardless of whether we have brothers or sisters -- that life carries each of us into our own particular worlds and impermeable solitudes? Is it because Lucius happily submitted to Benno's benevolent control, and who amongst us doesn't secretly crave the validation of that happy submission from our loved ones -- be they spouses or children or, as a last resort and most typically, a dog or a cat? When my great dog dies, I will surely get another one, and I will walk with him through the neighborhood, my hand connected to his neck by a leash. Sometimes, we'll go to the very polo fields of Benno's story, and I'll let my dog off his leash to run free. He'll romp about, graze in the horses' sweet pasture, nibble on their manure, and run to me smiling when I call. And when we get home, I'll feed him his food and water from steel bowls on the floor; and when I lay down on the couch to watch TV, he'll sit on the floor beside me; and when I go to bed at the end of the day and close my bedroom door, he'll sleep peacefully on the floor outside my room. For much of the day, I'll ignore him, but by the end of each day we will have exchanged more gestures of mutual affection than most pairs of people would.

A week to the day after I heard the end of Benno's story, I had a dream of my own. I don't often remember dreams, but this one I remembered. I had carried my kayak down to the river for a paddle. It was a summer afternoon, and the sun was hot. I dropped the kayak in, but rather than stepping into it and pushing off, I sat down in the shallow water. My rear end sunk down around six inches into the muddy bottom, and I reached my hands down on both sides of me and grabbed two cool handfuls of Chattahoochee River mud. I let the mud slide through my fingers, and then I lay down fully in the water, almost floating, barely touching the bottom, my eyes, nose and mouth all barely submerged, and my hands gently anchoring me to the mud. The river was all around me. Instead of me flowing over the water, I let the water flow over me. Clean water, branches and sticks, a beer can, leaves, bugs, fish, turtles, ducks, dog shit, a beaver, a small dead cat, Abraham Lincoln, more water, always more water, a deflated inner tube, Benno and Lucius, brown foam, my parents, the dead alpha buck with the arrow still lodged in him, my children holding hands with my future grandchildren, and more and more water, always flowing, more life, flowing and flowing without end. Eventually, I let go and drifted downstream like the rest. It felt good to just flow along. I woke up filthy clean.

"Except for a little more," I said. Around a year ago, a year after he had told me his story, Benno got married. He married Hazel, one of the lady residents. As he had said, he hadn't told the full story since he'd related it to the doctors upon his admission to the Home. Maybe he needed time, maybe he needed to tell it again, but he put his life with Lucius away for safe keeping and was able to move ahead. Benno and Hazel seemed genuinely charmed with each other. He asked me, his "ribeye," to officiate at the ceremony. I went online, got ordained as a minister of The Universal Life Church, and was proud to marry them. The ceremony was in the multipurpose room where I typically led services. We had probably a hundred residents in attendance, the biggest crowd I'd ever had there by far. The marriage was reason for hope. Maybe, I told the crowd, maybe one day *I'd* even try out marriage again. Maybe when I was ninety, maybe sooner. A couple of the saucier septuagenarians might have cast a hopeful glance in my direction; I couldn't be sure. But it wasn't of them I was thinking. Hope could keep me company. I was thinking of Hope.

Acknowledgements

I have received timely and thoughtful feedback in the drafting of this book from a small but keenly intelligent cadre of friends. These include Jay Myers, Sabrina Smith, Jeff Potash, Susan Hughes, Carranza Pryor, and Rebecca Lieberman (a friend who doubles as a sister). They have all helped me to see my own book more fully than I was able to see it myself, which was a great help in the final stages of drafting. They have also all duly noted potential criticisms I might receive. They are all hereby deemed to be pure and blameless! Any shortcoming of the book is mine.

The lovely cover art for the book is a literal gift from my friend, Ivan Reyes, whom I hereby thank, very, very much.

I would also like to thank my parents for their reading and feedback and encouragement. It's a bit late in life for me to start writing, but not once did they question the endeavor. On the other hand, my college aged children often questioned it, as they often question many or most things that I do. Their filial skepticism was its own kind of constructive criticism, which I valued. And as I hope they know, their love buoys me every day.

Made in the USA
Middletown, DE
10 September 2018